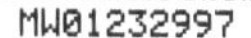

The Story of a Friendship

Gwen Morrison

PublishAmerica
Baltimore

First printing

ISBN: 1-4137-4586-5
PUBLISHED BY PUBLISHAMERICA, LLLP
www.publishamerica.com
Baltimore

Printed in the United States of America

Jessica
To "best" friends
and
best-for-now friends
Hugs
Gwen

Advance praise for

Friendship is an incredibly important part of a women's life. Studies have shown that women who have a good girlfriend have much better life coping skills and lead happier lives. Gwen Morrison's *Ivy* truly portrays the importance of friends. Through the pages of *Ivy*, Paige and Josie became my friends, as well. I shared in their laughter and their tears and felt like I made two new friends. Morrison's ability to bring a story to life was incredible and I can't wait to read more of her work.

—Tracy Lyn Moland, author of *Mom Management, Managing Mom Before Everybody Else*

Ivy: The Story of a Friendship sails through the seasons of life like an exquisite bird soaring beyond despair and regret, gliding above hope and thanksgiving, stopping only to gather twigs of joy and sips of understanding. It is a powerful journey that ventures to the very soul of forgiveness, by way of the heart. Don't miss it!

—J. L. Miles, author of *Roseflower Creek*

For Lisa, my dearest friend,
for being the instrument of my inspiration
and for believing in me, even when I didn't.
Forever friends are hard to find.
I'm glad I found you.

Acknowledgments

The pathway on the journey through our lives is filled with special people. They will either travel with us or point us in the right direction. I've been blessed to have many special people cross my path as I got to know the women in this novel.

Through the process of writing this novel, and in all of my adventures in the literary world and beyond, my sister Michelle has made me feel that I could overcome anything. Her confidence in me gives me courage. Even if I will always look twice, I'm thankful she's with me when I cross the road. Even big sisters need a hand to hold every now and then.

My thanks to Karen Ariail, a dear friend who I know will always be my biggest cheerleader. And to the other book club ladies who supported *Ivy* from the beginning.

Thank you to my parents for giving me the gift of imagination and to my sister Paula whose heart is as big as any I know.

A special thanks to Tracy Lyn Moland. Without her words of encouragement, this novel may have lived in my desk drawer forever.

My gratitude goes out to Victoria Zackheim, Marrion Barnes, Don and Gloria Stewart, J. L. Miles and Neva Watford, who were among my first readers. Thanks for your faith in me and in the story.

Thank you to my family: Dave, Tim, Robyn, Nicholas and Dylan. Without your patience and encouragement, this novel would never have been written. Thank you for your love and support in all things.

Thank you to the American Cancer Society for your continued support of cancer patients and those who love them.

Prologue

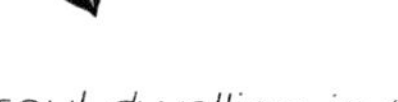

"Friendship is a single soul dwelling in two bodies."
—Aristotle

I stared at the words *Beloved Wife and Loving Mother.* Hardly. There was so much more. She was the best friend anyone could ask for, and she was mine. I crept in a little closer, touched the ornate letters that declared her identity. My fingers traced each syllable, willing them into my permanent memory: Josephine Marie Ferguson. I followed the trail of ivy carved into the beveled granite headstone. It took me a minute to realize why it was there and I smiled. She had put it there for me.

A few years back, Josie bought a book on symbolism. She was fascinated with learning new things, no matter how obscure, so she answered an advertisement that read: *Have you ever seen a symbol or abbreviation on a document and not known what it meant? Well, now you can learn. For just $29.95 we will provide you with the book that helps you decipher hundreds of hidden symbols.* Reading through the book one afternoon at the park, we were thrilled to discover the symbol for friendship. On the third page, under the category *Plant* was this:

Ivy: friendship and immortality.

There was ivy trailing down Josie's mountain-rose headstone and I knew what she was telling me.

The anger I had experienced the previous month started to melt away as I knelt before her headstone. The reality of the moment was rushing through my body, creating a cold aching in my bones. It was like a fast-moving disease spreading through my body. Josie was gone. All that was left of her was the stone marker adorning the ground in front of me, a marker stark and cold, so unlike the person whose name was engraved on its surface.

In the end, was that it?

I closed my eyes, remembering her cheerful voice, a voice I had heard every day, hoped I would not soon forget. "Good morning, Miss Paige," she would say. "How are you this morning? Get lucky last night?" These words, our talks, had become our morning ritual. We called it our House Fraus Early Morning Sex Talk. The sex talks were a little embarrassing at first because Josie spared no details. I sometimes found it difficult to look at her husband, Tom, especially after she described the time he slipped off the bed while climbing on top of her. "He thought he broke his winky!" she had laughed. "He kept checking it. It was so funny!" And the next day, I could barely contain myself when I noticed his tiny limp as he took the trash out to the curb. Finally, after all the years with Josie, nothing she said embarrassed me. At the same time, nothing was taboo with her. She was always trying to shock me, trying to get that pink flush to rise and color my cheeks.

The tears fell, as they had so many times in the past. But Josie wasn't here to dry them with her tattered blue dishtowel. I remember teasing her about that dishtowel.

"I can't throw it away, it still has some use." She held the old thing as if it were a treasured possession. "People throw things away too easily, don't ya think? Besides," she added. "Too many things in life are disposable."

Now I was alone with a throbbing pain, longing for her to come to me and, in Josie-fashion, tell me, "Come on, get over it. I know it hurts now, but life goes on. It's the cycle, chick. We live and we die; it's what we do with the living part that matters. Live while you can!"

Live while you can. My body started to tremble, my stomach burning. I put my hands to my chest, trying to slow the breathing. My heart was thumping so hard it felt as though it would come through my chest, broken and bleeding. So that's what it meant, "Poor girl, she died from grief." It really could happen.

I bent down and ran my hands through the soil. I needed her to tell me what I should do without her. She was the one with all the answers. Like the one time I was certain that I was going to leave Jason. I was convinced that he was the worst husband, because he forgot my birthday. It was Josie who, over a large pitcher of frozen margaritas, brought me to my senses. She had this easy understanding of the complex differences between men and women. They were beyond my comprehension. Josie understood men more than men understand men. Her motto was: *Men are just men, they can't help it.*

We were as different as could be; maybe that's what made us so close. She once told me that, between the two of us, we made the perfect woman. I remember how her hazel eyes sparkled when she ran down the list of her own good qualities. "Well, let's see, I'm creative, caring, and I have a great ass." She laughed. "That's always a good thing." As if to share this greatness with me, she strutted that ass across the room.

At the end of every year we sat around a roaring fire—usually in her backyard and layered in coats and blankets—and went over our most-improved list. We took turns remembering the year, talking only about our lives. Josie insisted on continuing the ritual, even when she was sick. She said it started the year off on a positive note and kept our memories clear of any negative baggage for the new year. Then we would break our glasses into the fire, sealing the end of one year, leaving all our troubles behind as we stepped into the next.

***

The sun was setting; the sky was a brilliant blaze of orange and red. The day was ending and a new one would begin, as though this one had never existed. Everything would be changed. I wasn't ready to let go. Not yet. I wanted this day to linger. I wanted the moon to slumber quietly, just a little longer.

Opening my straw purse, I toyed with the white envelope tucked inside. Josie's husband had dropped it by the house. I quickly closed my bag, leaving the letter tucked safely inside. I wasn't ready. The day was not over for me; I didn't want to let it end. I lay down and closed my eyes tight against the impending dusk.

A crackling sound brought me up from the sacred ground. Turning, I saw her and nodded, then smiled.

One

"It's the friends you can call up at 4 a.m. that matter."
—Marlene Dietrich

Paige

I added more hot water to the tub and leaned back to rest on my pink inflatable pillow. Heat from the tub rose and covered the big picture window with steam. I felt myself drifting away, the warmth making my eyelids heavy. Suddenly, the doorbell sounded in the hall below. I figured it was the paperboy looking for the thirteen bucks I owed him. He had this uncanny ability to show up every time I tried to take a bath. I don't know why we kept getting delivery, since the newspapers always ended up in the bushes, crumpled or wet.

It was impossible to ignore the incessant ringing, especially when it was soon accompanied by a knocking so loud that it seemed as if someone were kicking down the door.

Damn that kid! I heaved myself out of the tub and threw on the terry-cloth robe. Water from my hair trickled down my spine.

I rushed into the bedroom and peeked through the drawn blinds. There was no one on the walkway, but I couldn't see the top step from that angle. I hobbled down the stairs, my robe clutched tightly in my fist.

At the door, I pulled back the semi-sheer panels and found not the paperboy, but a woman. Unlocking the three locks, I opened the door. The woman was bent over.

I squinted against the bright morning sun. "Can I help you?"

She lifted her head and her eyes appeared to roll around in their sockets. She gripped an old coat around her middle and then stumbled forward, letting out the most gruesome, animalistic sound I had ever heard. It caused me to jump back. The door flew open as the woman crumpled to her knees, falling right into my foyer. She was breathing heavily, reaching for my robe. She used it to pull herself to her knees.

"Should I call someone for you?"

"Lady," she squealed. "I…am …having a *baby*!" And then she slumped back onto the polished hardwood floor.

"A baby? Oh, okay…a baby?" My mind was blank. "You mean right now? You're having a baby now?"

The woman gripped her stomach and screamed. I had never in my life heard such a sound come from a human. I had worked at a pet store and there was a horrible dog that whined in what sounded like a guttural moan. That was the sound this woman was making. I shivered, suddenly cold in my robe.

"Give me just a minute, okay? I'll be right back. Just wait here."

"Trust me, I'm not going anywhere," she said. "But hurry!"

I rushed up the stairs, threw on a pair of jeans and a sweatshirt, grabbed the keys to the Grand Am, and made my way back down to the stranger, who was now perched on the bottom step and making huffing sounds.

***

It was no easy feat, transporting the extremely pregnant woman from my front door to the car, but we managed.

"A two-door!" she shouted, throwing both arms up to the heavens. "Jesus, great."

I fumbled with the lock on the passenger door and the keys slipped out of my hand.

"Come on, lady! I'm about to drop my uterus right here in your pansy bed!" She clutched her stomach and spread her legs, as if to keep herself from toppling over.

I helped ease her swollen body onto the front seat, my temples pulsing to the rhythm of my pounding heart. Sweat dripped from my brow. As I drove over the curb, the woman let out a short grunt, followed by a fizzled squeak.

"Glad you upgraded to the leather seats, honey," she said between squeals. Her breathing was loud and heavy, her chest heaving. I found myself mimicking her movements—in and out, slow and easy—until my head started to spin.

"My husband hates cloth seats," I explained. "When we bought the car, this really rude salesman was trying to sell us on the luxury of cloth and all that, but..."

I looked over and the woman appeared to be fading fast. Her chin was on her chest and her dark hair was matted against the top of her head. "My water just broke," she said. "So you can tell your husband...leather... was...the right...choice."

I caught sight of the blue hospital sign. "Almost there," I said, and she grunted. I pressed harder on the accelerator, swung around the corner and spotted an abandoned wheelchair. I pulled into the circular drive and made a beeline for it. "Hold on, here we go."

"Yeah, I—Ahhhhh, shit!" She looked at me. "Sorry, but it really hurts." Her eyes filled with tears, a large pool teetering, just on the edge of spilling over.

"You're in good hands now," I said, killing the engine. "We'll get you inside and you'll have your baby." I rushed around to the passenger side, leaned in and put my arm around her shoulders. I eased her legs across the seat, got her into the wheelchair, and raced toward the entrance. I pushed her through the double doors into the crowded emergency waiting room and was more than relieved to see all those people in hospital gear. A quick explanation and they took over.

Done, I thought, *I did my part*. Now they can help her... Poor thing. What *does* amniotic fluid do to leather seats?

"Good luck," I told her. "You're in good hands now." I patted the woman on the shoulder and turned to leave.

"Are you the coach?" came a voice from behind me.

I turned. "Who me? No, no, I never. No, I don't, uh, no. Not me."

A familiar voice crackled behind the nurse. "Yep, that's my sis. Hubby's out of town, she's my backup." The stranger looked straight at me, her eyes reflecting what I could have sworn was fear.

"Great," said the blonde-haired and perky nurse. "We better get you into a gown so you can deliver this bundle of joy. By the sounds of it, you may be close." She grabbed the wheelchair and pushed it down the hall, her perfect ponytail bobbing behind her.

I felt my feet moving and saw the sign: *Delivery Room.*

"Here," said Nurse Perky. "Slide these over your clothes and we'll call you after we check to see how far she's dilated."

Dilated? Eek. I put on the green scrubs, the paper booties, and lunch-lady cap, and then plopped down onto a chair in the hallway. I didn't have to wait long.

***

The air in the delivery room was cold, probably so birthing coaches didn't faint. There was an odor I couldn't place; it was not pleasant. It fell somewhere between formaldehyde and stinky socks. *What in the hell am I doing here?* I thought. I wanted to dart from the room and crawl back into my warm tub, where I had been soaking away my worries. My eyes met the woman's and I knew that I wasn't going anywhere for quite a while. It was in that moment that I really looked at her for the first time and her eyes were silently pleading *Stay, please stay.*

I shifted on the circular stool, repositioning myself into a semi-comfortable position, and then I reached out and touched her hand, rubbed it. It had an unfamiliar feel, this hand of a stranger. Her short fingers were ice-cold and her nails jagged. For a moment I thought she was grinning at me, but then her face contorted, she clenched my hand, inhaled deeply and held her breath.

"Bear down, push, there you go, now four, five, six, seven. Okay, good, now breathe—relax, good, that's a girl." The woman had obviously taken lessons on this birthing thing, because she was settling into the rhythm. Her brow glistened with sweat and she bore down. I found myself scrunching up my face and holding my breath along with her. Hours seemed to pass as she labored, pushing and breathing, breathing and pushing.

"Ah! God damn it, that hurts! Oh, I can't do it!" A stray tear slid down her face. "Let me get up!" she hollered. "I don't want to do this anymore!"

Her grip tightened around my hand until my fingers were drained of all noticeable color. I let her squeeze, even though my wedding ring already felt as if it were imbedded in my finger.

"Shit!!! Tom! I can't do this! I—ahhhh—fuck!"

Suddenly, the room seemed frigid again and a shiver ran through me. I glanced around, searching for something to distract me from this screeching and the cold. I hummed under my breath. Don't they tell you to focus on one specific object? Or was that just for the mother?

The mirror above the doctor's head caught my eye. It was positioned in a way that displayed the entire birth scene, in living color. My eyes froze on the unfolding drama, a cross between a horror movie and one of those late-night medical documentaries. I was waiting for the doctor to start identifying the gruesome object that was slipping from the woman on the table. A gray, dark thing, bloody and pulsing, was emerging from between her legs. I couldn't tell if it was the baby or the afterbirth that I'd seen on those reality shows. The woman was totally oblivious, caught up in panting, breathing and yanking on my arm. Her hair was now completely matted to her forehead; she looked exhausted. Letting go of my hand, she leaned forward and gave one huge push. Her face turned, as if she were going to explode. Her chest heaved and a low rasping sound escaped from her throat, starting out loud and hissing, like a balloon that has been blown up and released. Spent, she collapsed back onto the bed and reached for my hand.

A gurgled cry suddenly filled the tiny room. I stood, wanting to get a better look as they lifted the baby. It was a boy. The *thing* in the mirror was a baby boy. It was over. A new baby and a new mother were in the room with me. I exhaled, not realizing that I had been holding my breath.

"You have a baby boy," I whispered, brushing away a tear that trickled down my cheek.

The woman nodded slowly, her eyes still closed.

"Look, here he is," I said, as they brought the swaddled baby to her chest.

The woman's eyes popped open. "Oh my God!" she said. "What the hell's wrong with his face?"

The baby was coated in a white, slimy film. Beneath it you could see where the birth had left its mark on the tiny wrinkled face.

"He's beautiful," assured the nurse. "The scratches will go away in a day or two and his features will pop up in less than a week. You did a wonderful job."

I felt a tug at my sweatshirt. "Is he ugly? You can tell me." She started to shake.

I looked into her bloodshot eyes. "He's the most beautiful baby boy I've ever seen," I told her. "He must take after his father." I'm sure I saw a smile.

The new mother lay back, giving my hand one last squeeze. I pulled the warmed blanket over the two of them, mother and son.

Two

"Since there is nothing so well worth having as friends, never lose a chance to make them."
—Francesco Guicciardini

It was weeks later when I spotted the woman again, getting out of a car parked in the driveway across the road. I watched as she carried the bundle—probably the new baby—into the Quigleys' house.

Mr. Quigley had to be almost ninety by now, the dear man. Maybe this was his long-lost granddaughter. I turned my attention back to checking out the tiny sprouts that would someday, hopefully, be a tulip garden. Spring was just around the corner. "Hey, you!" a voice sounded behind me. I strained my neck around and toppled onto the damp grass. Before I could recover, the woman was at my side, baby in arms.

"How are you feeling?" I said, struggling to my feet and brushing at the dampness on my backside. "I never did get your name—not that there was time in all the excitement."

The woman chuckled. "Can you believe it? You rescue me from giving birth right on the driveway and here we are, strangers. I'm Josie," she said. "Josephine Marie Ferguson. But please, call me Josie. I don't know what the hell my mother was thinking when she came up with Josephine. I swear, the woman read too many of those romance novels. What was so wrong with Karen or Lisa? Or Melissa. I always thought

I looked more like a Melissa. By the way," she added with a bright smile and pointing to the house across the street. "We're the new neighbors."

My eyes followed where she was pointing. " I didn't even know the house had sold."

"It was my husband's uncle's house; he's not living there anymore. It was too much to handle for the old guy. Anyway, he left most of his stuff there, like his ninety-year-old couch and his eighty-five-year-old kitchen table."

I noticed how her face softened, how she shifted her weight from one hip to the other, balancing the new baby on her shoulder. She looked so comfortable, natural, and I wondered if they taught you how to hold babies when they let you bring them home. For some women, motherhood was something they tried on and found to be a perfect fit. The thought caused a familiar stir deep within me and I quickly dismissed it. Josie was still reciting all the furniture that had been left in the house and I looked across the road. I hadn't realized how much the place had deteriorated. A few years back, when Jason went over to review the old man's will, I tagged along. I hadn't seen Mr. Quigley for some time. He always liked my cookies; the one thing I did well in the kitchen. Even then, his house was in desperate need of an overhaul. As Josie spoke, I recalled that floral wallpaper with the shiny gold trim. It was plastered on most of the walls and would drive me crazy in a day. When she was finished with her list, I smiled. "Well then, welcome to the neighborhood. Had I known, I could have made you a quiche or something."

Josie waved her free hand back and forth in front of her as though she were swatting at flies. "A quiche? Girl, you did a hell of a lot more than the Welcome Wagon Lady would've done."

I felt my face get hot and focused on adjusting the straps on my overalls. I had a momentary flashback of the whole delivery scene and tried hard not to look at her.

"I know it was a really crazy thing, me showing up on your doorstep like that, so I had to come and say thanks. And, of course tell you who I was. That night, your light was the only one on, so you were the lucky winner."

I took off my gardening gloves and brushed soil from my hands. "Well, no problem. How's the baby doing?" Josie pulled back the soft blue blanket and I peeked in at the sleeping infant. His face was crumpled like an old man's, but he looked a lot better than the first time I saw him. *What a miracle this is,* I thought.

"You mean *the thing*?" She smiled, looking down at her sleeping son.

I looked up, confused.

"That *is* what you called him when he was being born. I wasn't *that* out of it," Josie said, laughing. "You said, and I quote, 'God, look at that thing!'"

I wasn't sure if I should laugh or cry. I didn't realize I had said it out loud. How awful! "Did I? I'm sorry, it was my first time watching another woman— well, you know, coaching and everything. I'm sorry. So what did you name him?" I dug the toe of my sneaker into the damp grass.

Josie shook her head. "It's fine, I'm just teasing you. You'll get used to it." She winked at me. "We called him Christopher, after my brother. He died in a motorcycle accident last year." Josie's eyes reflected a still-fresh sadness. "I didn't get your name, either, in all the confusion. And did I ever say thank you? Really, I can't thank you enough for taking care of us the way you did."

"Sorry, I'm Paige. Paige Matthews. And it was my pleasure. Really, I'm really glad I was there."

"Have you lived here long?" asked Josie, peering behind me, her eyes alighting on the unkempt mound of dirt that I hoped would one day resemble a magnificent garden oasis.

"We bought the house the year we got married, so I guess it's been about six years. It was a fixer-upper, to say the least. We've done a lot inside; now I'm hoping to do some work outside, like this garden." I pointed to my work-in-progress. "It's sad; I just don't have a green thumb. Everything I plant dies."

Josie scanned the mound of dirt that I'd been spreading out below the front window. "You're in luck. My maiden name was Stewart. No relation to Martha, but I can create wonders in the dirt." She looked ready to jump in and start digging.

"That's wonderful!" I said. "I may have to call on you for some serious advice, as soon as the frost breaks. I read online about new topsoil and thought I better get started soon."

"Paige, I'm pretty sure I owe you at least one," laughed Josie. "I think it was tough after his wife died. He just gave up, and the house really suffered. It's a disaster."

I glanced at the house. It wasn't big, but none of the houses on this street were. Three bedrooms, a front porch, and they usually had only one bath. Not at all like the newer neighborhoods here, in Des Moines, where some houses have four and five bedrooms and three bathrooms. "It needs some TLC," I said, "but you'll make it your own soon."

Josie nodded. "Yeah, I will. Did you know him well?" She pointed at Mr. Quigley's house. "His wife did everything for him. She even ironed his underwear. Can you believe it?" Josie said. "I would never do that for Tom. Tom's my husband. Not that I don't love him, don't get me wrong, but come on, ironing underwear?"

I laughed at Josie, this new neighbor standing on my lawn and proclaiming her independence from ironing her husband's underwear. Her face was flushed; she was clutching a new baby, and staring fixedly at me, waiting for my response.

"Well, no, I can't say as I've ever ironed underwear for anyone," I said, choking back a giggle.

"Thank God!" Before I could respond, she rushed ahead. "I was afraid for a minute that you might be one of those Holly Housewife types who dotes on her husband's every whim. You know, the ones who wait patiently at the door every evening, beer in hand, greeting the master of the house as he arrives home from work? Ick! There would just be no way this friendship could work if you were."

I wouldn't call myself Holly Housewife, but I did like to greet Jason when he got home. I wasn't about to tell my new neighbor that. Instead, I said, "Yeah, I know the type. Thank God we're not like that. I don't even cook. Jason does all the cooking. He loves it, and that works for me. It's not that I can't cook," I quickly added. "But he's the experimental one. Like last night, he made this awesome coq au vin thing. It's a French chicken dish," I told her.

Josie shrugged. "Never had that before. The only Coke I know comes in a can. And what is vin? Doesn't that mean wine or something?"

"Beats me, but it was amazing," I said. "Hey, maybe we can have you and your family over for dinner? Jay loves to show off his culinary prowess whenever he gets a chance."

"I'll take you up on that, as long as you don't use the word *prowess* ever again," Josie said, shaking her head. "What the hell is prowess?" We both laughed. It had been a while since I'd enjoyed such an easy conversation with another woman. But why was I trying so hard to impress her?

"It'll be a while before our house is fit for company," she said. "I'm hoping to get the floral paper off the walls this week. Care to come help out?"

I hesitated for a moment. "Love to. Might be fun. I have to work on Monday, but Tuesday is free."

"Great! It's a date. Bring along something to scrape with and a spray bottle and maybe, just maybe, we can find some bare wall under all those damn daffodils." Josie rolled her eyes. The baby started to stir and she patted him softly on the back.

"Sounds good to me," I said. "Anything else I can bring? Do you have everything you need? Do you know where all the stores are?"

Josie nodded slowly. "Yep, we lived here about six years ago, then moved to Florida for my husband's job. This is more home to me than Florida ever was. Too damn hot there, and way too many old people. Someone told me it was God's waiting room, so I took that as my cue to leave." She shifted her weight again. "Well, I need to get some exercise and wallpaper removal is a start." Josie patted her swollen stomach with her free hand. "This, I can do without."

"You look great," I said. "Especially for someone who just had a baby. It's funny," I added. "I don't remember seeing a moving truck. When did you move in, anyway?"

"Our stuff's in storage. It's a long story; so don't even ask. We have to wait 'til the guy comes back from vacation to get all our stuff. The place is furnished and everything, so it's no big deal, but I can't wait to really make it mine. You know how it is, right? It's just not home 'til you have pictures of your family hanging around."

I nodded. My home was my haven; my whole life was in my house. "I bet it's tough. I work out of my house, so I know how important it is to be comfortable in your home. I would hate to feel like I didn't belong yet. You'll make it your own soon enough." *I'm giving this woman advice now. What am I doing?*

Josie patted the blue blanket. "Could be worse. I'm just happy to be back where we belong." The baby squirmed again. "I'd better let you get back to what you were doing; time for me to feed the leech. The way this kid sucks, I'm sure to be down a bra size in a month!"

"Yikes! It was nice to finally talk to you, you know. I'll see you next week." The sun was starting to go down behind Josie's house. I didn't realize we'd been chatting so long.

"Sure thing, can't wait." She turned and walked a few steps, and then turned back. "Paige, I'm not a mushy kind of person, you'll find out soon enough, but I don't know if I'll ever be able to thank you enough for helping me. I was so scared that night. More than you could even imagine. Tom was working and I couldn't reach him, and I didn't know anyone in the neighborhood and, well, just thanks."

I met her gaze and saw a tear forming at the corner of her eye.

"Glad you found me," I said, nodding.

Josie turned and rushed back across the road as quickly as she came. Heading up her walk, she swatted the weeping willow branches out of her way just as the sun slipped behind her house.

Three

"The ornament of a house is the friends who frequent it."
—Ralph Waldo Emerson

All the lights were off and the shades were drawn when I walked into Josie's house, and it was only two in the afternoon. That was usually a sign that she was trying to get Christopher to take his afternoon nap, so I really wasn't surprised. She had told me earlier in the day to just come in, so the doorbell wouldn't awaken him, and that he had been fighting it for the last few weeks, which was not sitting well with her. Tired from getting up all hours of the night to feed him, she told me she relished the short time he did sleep during the day.

The flickering candle on top of the mantel offered me just enough light to make my way over to the leather sofa. The combination of quiet and this dancing candlelight created an aura of tranquility in the tiny room. My eyes closed as I rested my head on the back of the couch to wait for my friend.

The shrill alarm of the telephone broke the silence, awakening me from my brief afternoon nap. On the third ring, I decided to pick it up.

"Ferguson residence. Hello?" I whispered. Click. I stood and stretched. Thinking that the caller might try again, I decided to check on Josie. It felt like I'd been asleep for hours. I tried to focus my eyes on my watch, but the numbers were blurry.

I made my way down the dimly lit hallway. Running my hand along the wall, I felt the sharp edges of the remains of the wallpaper we had started stripping. Once we got going, there was no end. It had taken us six whole months to find the bare walls. Josie was not discouraged. In fact, ever patient, she always seemed to find adventure and worth in every mundane thing we did together. It amazed me.

"It's like uncovering layers of history," she said, a wet piece of pink wallpaper stuck to her forehead. "Maybe there's a secret message underneath all this guck. Or initials of two young lovers carved in the wall as a memory of their undying love. Or a child's first drawing in her new house. Who knows what treasure we'll uncover—now pull!"

When I suggested we were more likely to reveal twelve layers of wet, stinky, moldy wallpaper, she shook her head and called me "O Pessimist Extraordinaire."

"Where's your imagination, girl? This old house has stories to tell," she said. "You just have to listen. Can't you hear the whispers?" She started going in circles, arms outstretched. "I feel them, don't you?" She lightly swept her fingers across my shoulders.

"You are officially nuts!" I said, giving her a swat on the arm.

Josie carefully pulled at the layers, while I ripped and shredded as much as I could, as fast as I could. What I discovered underneath was pretty much what I'd predicted. No matter how dramatic I wanted to be, wallpaper-turned-to-mush just didn't do it. And try as I could, I never did find the romance in the tedious job of wallpaper stripping. However, I was doing it with Josie, which made it fun.

I reached the end of the dark hall and I peeked in the doorway of the nursery. Josie was standing over the crib staring down at her son. The fresh scent of baby powder filled my senses. It always smells like innocence to me, its scent a hallmark for newness and purity.

Josie turned and caught sight of me.

"Finally," she whispered, quietly closing the door to Christopher's room. She flicked on the lights as she moved through the house. "I can't believe it took him this long. I think I've ruined him." She paused. "I really think I have."

"Ruined him how?" I asked, following her into the living room.

"By rocking him to sleep all the time. This book I bought over the

Internet says you shouldn't rock your baby to sleep, that you should just let him cry it out, but I just can't stand to hear his little sobs." Josie stretched out on the Berber carpet. "Those pitiful little peeping sounds he makes, it kills me. And then if he cries too long—God, it's friggin' pathetic. He makes that funny, hesitating little cry, it's just too sad."

"You're more of an expert than I am," I said. "We can't even get to the pregnancy stage, so you're asking the wrong person for parenting advice."

Her face softened. "God, Paige, I'm sorry. How is that going, or should I ask?"

I exhaled, blowing the hair off my face. "It's not easy. We've been trying for almost two years…and nothing. I want to go and see someone, but you know Jason." I didn't need to say anything more. Josie nodded. "We discussed this issue so many times and it was always the same. Jason refuses to accept that there might be something 'wrong' with us. He wants to wait. And wait. He claims it's stress, or work, or just timing. He can't face the fact that maybe, just maybe, one of us is not perfect." *If he only knew how imperfect I really was.*

"Paige, you have to check it out. It's a long time to be trying. Anyway, that's what that book says. Here, let's check." Josie hauled out the almost six-hundred-page pregnancy book that she said was her bible when she was pregnant with Christopher. She sifted through the front pages of *The Mother of All Pregnancy Books* and hesitated. "Here it is: 'Studies have shown that couples who haven't conceived after two years of trying have a one-in-four chance of conceiving without medical assistance.'"

"Hey, thanks, just what I came over for: a little encouragement to go with that coffee you still haven't made me." I shifted in my seat, uncomfortable that she knew so much about me. At the same time, I was grateful that she knew so much about me. I had never had an adult best friend. We were really starting to click. In the past, I had shied away from the traditional female friendships, not wanting to share the intimate details of my life. I was even less inclined to listen to the sordid details of other women's lives. With Josie, however, it felt different. Even with our quirky beginning, I found myself turning to her more and more. It felt good to have someone to laugh with; someone who was willing to listen to my complaints without putting a hand up. Jason put up his hand—like a stop sign—whenever I started talking about my feelings about having a baby. He said we talked about it so much that it was no wonder we couldn't get pregnant.

"So, you want coffee?" When I raised my eyebrow, she said, "Why didn't you just say so?" She set the book on the table.

The truth is, I could have read all about infertility, but there wasn't anything in there I didn't already know. I was tired of reading about it. I was tired of talking about it. I was tired of being a statistic in a damn infertility chapter.

"Is it too early for alcohol?" I smiled and glanced at my watch. It was already three-thirty and we had not stripped one sheet of wallpaper from the bathroom. (This explains why it had taken us six months to finish the dining room.)

"If I drink anything, I might just fall dead asleep right here and then we won't get anything done. How about coffee with just a shot of something from the top cupboard?" Her offer came with a wicked smile. The "top cupboard" had been a friend to us on many evenings, as we sat on the floor, side by side, chatting about everything from our first period to our first sexual experience. It became clear, after just a short time, that nothing was taboo in our conversations. Well, almost nothing.

"You're on. But not that crème du menthe stuff, that was horrible. Tasted like peppermint gum!"

"I've got just the thing to liven up your cuppa java," she said, and sneaked away to concoct her secret potion. Josie liked to tell what she put in it *after* I tasted it. She claimed to have been a bartender in her youth, but from what I tasted, I wasn't convinced. The one thing she did make was a killer margarita, calling it her love potion. She swore that if I drank three in a row, I'd be pregnant that very night.

Josie brought the coffee into the living room and we sat in silence sipping the hot brew. I held the cup with both hands, breathing in the sweet aroma. Irish cream, definitely. My thoughts were on making a baby. Rather, on not being able to make a baby. The last months had been so hard. Every time my period was a day late, my heart started to celebrate. And then, a day or two later I'd feel the familiar cramping and elation was snatched away. I didn't even feel like working because I was totally consumed by my biological clock. It ticked louder and louder every month.

"So, really, do you want to talk about it?" she asked, picking up on my darkening mood.

"I just thought it would be easy," I said. "It's easy for most everyone else I know, so why not for me?" I hesitated for a moment, unsure of continuing. I've never been good at revealing my feelings. But this was Josie, my friend. "It's just that I feel like such a failure. I know I'm not the only one, but it's so draining, you know? And I can't think of anything else, it's on my mind every moment."

I knew that the dining room was the next place Josie wanted to tackle and I asked if we were ever going to get to it. "And have you picked out the new pattern for the hallway yet?" Both of us knew that I was changing the subject, but I was feeling so defeated.

Josie looked at me for a moment. "No, sweetie, I haven't had time. Christopher is still so fussy and you know that Tom's no help. Men just are so useless sometimes. At least my man is, anyway. I wouldn't dream of trying to wallpaper with him. We'd end up divorcing if we tried to be in the same space for too long. He enjoys his sports on TV and his poker nights; I enjoy the decorating, my quiet time with Christopher, and spending time with girlfriends. It works for us, this being 'separate, yet together,'" Josie stood and cleared the coffee cups. "I love the guy, but men are men. I can't explain it. They're a different species, that's for sure. I mean, it never dawns on him to do certain things, so I just end up doing them myself. I know he'd do it if I asked, but if I have to do that—well, forget it."

"Ah, come on," I protested. "I've seen Tom and he's more of a helper than my husband will ever be. You wouldn't catch Jay on a ladder clearing the leaves from the eaves." I laughed. "He's great at cooking and that's about it. If he saw a dirty sock walking down the hallway, he wouldn't be surprised. I'm sure he thinks they walk to the laundry room by themselves, throw themselves into the washing machine, and then waltz back into his drawer."

Just then, I heard the faint squeak of a baby—the little man was awake.

"Uh-oh! What time is it?" I panicked and jumped off the couch, nearly knocking over the little oak table, along with the toy radio perched on top of it. "I have to run, Jo. Tonight's the night I cook." I really hated cooking, but it was the least I could do when I had a day off.

"So what's it going to be, chicken…or chicken? Hey, how about chicken!" Josie always laughed at my love of chicken, and it was the only thing I cooked well. So why ruin a good thing? "Actually, I announced with a grin, "tonight we are having chicken *and* rice."

"Ah, Minute Rice?" Josie already knew that this would be my rice of choice. Not the fancy rice that Jay prepares—balsamic or basmatic or something that ends in "ic" and tastes wonderful. If it were Jason's night to cook, he would have prepared teriyaki chicken, fancy rice and steamed asparagus.

"But of course," I teased. "Only the best. Hey, how long does that take to cook Minute Rice, anyway?"

"Funny. I'm pretty sure it only takes a minute, but with you, well, you never know." She scooped Christopher into her arms, wiped his tiny nose on her T-shirt, and walked me back to the door.

"Same time tomorrow?" Josie asked. "And I promise we'll do something with the wallpaper. I know you are dying to get your hands all gluey again. Hey, do you think we could sneak out next week and buy the paper? It's payday on Friday and I gotta get to it before I spend it on something useful—like groceries or the gas bill."

"Let's talk about it tomorrow," I said. With one foot out the door, I remembered something. "I have to work in the morning, so I may be a little late." Taking a breath, I added, "And thanks for the chat, Josie. I'll keep you posted on our conception activity." I grinned at Christopher, all wet and pink from his nap.

"Best of luck with your bird," she said.

I turned, confused.

"Your chicken. Boy, you have a very dirty mind. How come I never knew that about you?" Josie laughed.

Four

"To live is so startling it leaves little time for anything else."
—Emily Dickinson

The morning sky was as overcast as my mood. I woke up and immediately felt the familiar stickiness between my legs. Another month, another failure.

Standing in the shower, I let the hot water pelt my face; tears sprang to my eyes. Is there a God? Is He punishing me?

I shut off the water, threw on a soft robe, and headed down to the kitchen and my coffeepot. I was barely around the corner when the phone rang.

"Hey! Good morning!" came the ever-perky voice at the other end. It was barely seven and Josie usually didn't call until at least seven-fifteen. I pictured her standing there in that yellow, sunny kitchen (with no wallpaper), dressed in her favorite jeans and a tight T-shirt. Her brunette hair was tucked neatly behind her ears and she had on the faintest amount of makeup—the brand that Victoria Principal wore. Josie saw it on the Shopping Channel and swears it makes her look at least five years younger.

"Yeah, hi," was all I could manage. I was hoping that once the caffeine worked its way into my bloodstream I'd get a jump-start on the day…and on my mood.

"You okay?" she asked. A pause. "I'll be right there." Click. In less than ten minutes, Josie and Christopher were standing in the front entrance witnessing my breakdown. Josie set Christopher down on the carpet and surrounded me with her arms. I laid my head on her shoulder. It felt so wonderful to be comforted, even for a minute. She smelled like ginger. I mentioned this to her before, asking whether it was a soap or a perfume that she used. "No idea," she had said. "I don't have anything that is ginger-ish. Weird. You sure it's not baby vomit?"

"I'm sorry," Josie said, as she stroked my hair. I pulled away, took a breath and headed back to the coffeepot for another jolt. Grabbing Josie's favorite Hooters coffee mug, I filled it to the brim. Cream and two sugars.

"Remember when we found this silly mug," she said, trying to humor me. "That dirty old man. Remember? He must've had thirty of them. Oh, well. Now, when people come over, they think you worked there." She winked at me. I managed to turn up the corner of my mouth—an almost-smile.

I set the cup down in front of her and turned it so the pink nipples weren't staring at me across the table. Thank God we didn't buy the creamer! It was hideous. As it was, I kept Josie's cup as far back in the cupboard as I could. She refused to take it home, claiming that her husband would like it *way* too much and she would never see it again.

"Okay. I came to take you for donuts. And I won't take no for an answer. You need some serious chocolate in your veins, girl."

I wrinkled up my nose and slumped back in the chair. Rubbing my eyes. "Can't. I think I might just go back to bed." I slumped farther down in the chair. I know Josie probably thought I was enjoying my misery a little too much.

"No way…you are not going back to bed. You're going for donuts. Now go! Hurry up…come on, please…get dressed. I'm starving and I need sugar! And Christopher hasn't even eaten yet. He is a growing boy. You want to deprive my child of a 'real' blueberry muffin? You want that on your conscience?"

Thank God for Josie. It had been almost a year since Josie moved in and I could barely remember my life without her in it. It's weird how we don't know what we are missing in our lives until we have it. Then we wonder how it was we didn't realize how badly we needed it.

"No, really. I'm fine," I said, grabbing a tissue and baring my teeth in a fake smile. "I was just kidding. I'm not going back to bed. I need to get it together. Anyway, I have a lady coming in an hour to get a perm." My salon in the basement had been set up a few years back and I was finally starting to have "regulars."

"A blue-hair? Which one? Is it the nice one from last week who brought those brownies, or is it that lady with four fingers?"

"What? Who are you talking about?" I asked, trying to remember my recent customers. I usually had the same ladies each week, mostly the elderly women from the neighborhood. They liked the convenience of walking to their hairdresser's house. The only problem was that I couldn't ever get them to leave. They wanted to sit and chat and eat brownies with me all day. It was sweet, really.

"That one...you know...you gave her that pinkish color on her hair a few weeks ago?" She looked at me, searching for some sign of recognition. I was blank.

"Oh...you know what? I dreamt that!" Josie went into fits of laughter. She was always having bizarre dreams and sometimes she wasn't sure if they really happened or not. One time she swore up and down that she and I had visited this particular restaurant around the corner. She even rattled off some of the conversations we allegedly had during our elaborate meal at the Pleasant Pheasant Restaurant—and except for the fact that we had never stepped foot in the place, it sounded pretty fun. She and I argued about it forever. She said I was wearing my black dress, my gold necklace with the tiny heart on it, and hoop earrings. My shoulder-length blonde hair was pinned up and I had on my favorite high-heeled shoes. Sounded good to me. Too bad it was a dream. I could use a night out on the town.

Josie was still giggling at the thought of her dream. I was sure she would spare me no details when she described my encounter with the four-fingered lady. Maybe this is what motherhood did to you. Once a functioning human being, now a woman who forgets to put on her shoes before leaving the house, talks in a tone that is just one octave above a normal tone and has an imagination that some would say is downright scary.

"Okay. Never mind. I can tell you later. I gotta go and eat something before I collapse," she said, scooping up Christopher, who had removed all my pots and pans from the kitchen cabinets.

"Thanks though," I said. "I'm okay now, really. This is just my thing. I have to figure out what to do now. Crying isn't going to do it. We'll talk later?"

She turned at the doorway. "Absolutely!" Josie rushed across the street. It was then that I noticed she was still wearing her furry pink slippers. I stared after her, daydreaming of the day when I would hold my baby. Would that day ever come, or had I missed my only chance?

***

The office was located on the north side of the city, where new buildings had recently been constructed. They looked so cold and hard, with not a single flower planted in the vast lawn area at the front. That was it, green and gray. Jason's office was around the corner, but I was on my own. I hadn't even told him when I made the appointment with Dr. Peterson.

The lobby was decorated in commercial-grade patterned carpet, reminding me of the yellow brick road. I imagined Josie's reaction to the eclectic design, how she would hop from square to square, without regard for the dozens of people who milled about. The rectangular shapes led the visitors from one impersonal beige door to another, each with a *Dr.* Somebody posted on it. I passed them—*Doctor of Podiatry*, *Doctor of Optometry*—and came to a door that said *Doctor of Obstetrics and Gynecology*. Gynecology. The word sounded as cold as the speculum that would soon be probing inside me.

There was an elderly receptionist seated at a desk behind a glass partition. She slid one of the panels to the side. "Please sign in here, dear," she said. "Are you a new patient?" I nodded, looking around the waiting room at pregnant women in varied gestational states.

"Insurance, driver's license, Social Security card, and twenty dollars for co-pay, please."

"Anything else?" I asked, handing her half the contents of my wallet.

She slid a bunch of papers through the window. "Just fill out these four forms, front and back, and then bring them back here when you're done. The doctor is running a little behind, so take your time, dear."

Great, four pages of paperwork. There was nothing worse than filling out your life story a dozen times. Every year my family doctor has his patients fill out the same forms. Every year. You would think they could upload or download or scan or whatever one does for the insurance companies. Was this not the age of technology?

The first page was easy—name, address, phone number, emergency contact, and all that personal stuff. I wiped my hands on my jeans, leaving a damp imprint on my leg. The second page asked you to write your medical history since the moment you arrived in this world.

After I completed the stack of paperwork, I deposited it on the receptionist's desk, sat down, and thumbed through a pile of crumpled, outdated magazines.

More than an hour later, a nurse appeared in the doorway. "Ms. Matthews? The doctor will see you now," she announced. Groggy, I followed her to the last door on the left.

"The ladies' room is right there across the hall. There are sample cups on the back of the toilet and please put your name on it *before* you use it. You can leave it on the ledge when you're done." Her tone was rehearsed. "Then you can come back in here and remove everything from the waist down—there's a sheet on the table to cover up with. The doctor won't be long." Famous last words; they all say that. I've often thought that male doctors should be forced to sit half naked for an hour, in their own examining rooms, and under the stark fluorescent lights, at least once a month, in order to appreciate how uncomfortable it is for us women. And why do they have the air conditioning set at a frigid sixty degrees, knowing we are bare-assed in here?

I peed in the cup and stripped down. To my surprise, there was a knock on the door just as I settled onto the table.

"How are you doing today?" asked the doctor, his bushy gray eyebrows moving up and down in a cartoon-like way, making me even more leery of the whole visit. "So, what are we here for, your annual check-up?"

I straightened my back. "Yes, that, and I need to talk to someone about fertility problems."

He nodded. "Let's get the hard part over with, and then we can sit and chat. How's that?" He was already shining the metal speculum that looked like a vice grip. "Just lay back—yes, scoot your bottom forward, knees bent a little—good. This is going to be a little cold, so relax, just a little pinch and...there."

How can a male doctor have any idea how horrible it feels to have this hard metal contraption shoved inside your vagina? I suppressed the urge to contract my leg and kick him in the head.

"All done," he told me, sliding out the speculum. "Easy as pie. You can sit up now." He pulled off the latex gloves and rinsed his hands in the miniature sink.

I repositioned the paper gown to cover my bare legs.

"Now, what else can I do for you today, young lady?"

I took a deep breath. "Well, my husband and I have been trying for more than two years to have a baby. I have regular cycles, so I don't know if there's a real medical problem." I had been going to another doctor for these annual visits, but she quit her practice to have a baby. It was weird talking to a man about this.

The doctor was squinting at the pages I filled out in the waiting room. "I see here that you had one pregnancy. Was it a live birth?"

Tears sprang to my eyes instantly. "Yes." I swallowed hard. "I was young and I gave the baby up. She was—" *She was beautiful*, that's what I really wanted to say. Though the nurses had tried to whisk her away before I could see her, I was watching and I saw her round little face, the tuft of blonde hair on the top of her tiny head. I saw her mouth opening like a little bird, searching, searching for her mother. I didn't remember any of this when I was with Josie, no memory of pain or blood. Just the beautiful baby girl.

"It's okay, dear, go on," he said, bringing me back to the present.

"She was adopted by a great family, so I was told. Anyway, I was fifteen and I couldn't keep her."

The doctor just stared, waiting for me to continue. I rubbed my arms to warm them. I felt my heart starting to pound and my chest tighten. *I couldn't keep her.* She was evil, my aunt had said. She would have brought evil into our family. I lifted my head and looked into his eyes. "I was raped," I blurted out. "My husband doesn't know."

To my surprise, the old doctor placed his hand on my shoulder. "Let's take this one step at a time; one thing may have nothing to do with the other."

I adjusted the blanket to cover more of my body, feeling very naked again. "What do I do first? How do I know if I'm okay?"

"I'll run a few tests and then we can meet again in a couple of weeks." His eyes seemed warmer than when I first saw them. "In the meantime, I think you might want to consider discussing your past with your husband; he does have a stake in all this and he should know. The problem may not be with you, but to reach a conclusive diagnosis of infertility, I may need to run tests on both of you." He stood to leave. "Go ahead and get dressed and I'll make arrangements for the tests and have the nurse call you with the details."

I sat there a while longer before putting on my clothes. My thoughts were on the little girl. The one with the big, beautiful eyes. I know she saw me too.

Five

"The truth is rarely pure and never simple."
—Oscar Wilde

Can you hand me the lettuce, sweetheart?" asked Jason as he chopped up the last of the vegetables for his famous "anything goes" salad.

"Is there anything you need help with?" I handed him the three kinds of lettuce he had bought at the market. Before I met Jason, I never even knew that lettuce came in different kinds. "I feel like I need to do something. Should I stir the sauce or something?"

"Paige, you know I like to do this alone; I'm in my element here. Maybe you could set the table? What time are the Fergusons coming?" he asked, chopping and tossing the salad like a pro.

I looked at the clock hanging above the window. "I think I told her five-thirty. Does that sound right?" I barely remembered inviting them. The week had been a total blur after leaving the doctor's office.

"How would I know?" he said. "You invited them, not me."

I sensed a little something in his voice. It was sharp, cutting. He always cleared his throat when he was getting irritated with me, like his personal version of counting to ten, or taking a deep breath.

Jason turned around to look at me. His piercing blue eyes had a yellow glint to them. "I just wanted to know what time to get everything ready," he said. "I'm sorry, I didn't mean to snap at you. But you know how important it is for me to pay attention when I'm cooking."

Grabbing the silverware, I left the kitchen and began setting the table for our guests. Christopher was going to be staying with a babysitter, so it was an adult evening. It had been months since just the four of us had done anything together. The last time had been kind of a bust. Tom had wanted to check out a new sports bar and we tagged along. The place was a little smoky and loud, but Jason had spent the entire night complaining about the smell. He sniffed his clothes every ten minutes until I finally thought it best to leave. It was a total disaster. Josie didn't care, she could have fun in a toxic waste pit, but I cared. My husband could be such an ass.

The sound of the doorbell broke my trance. I set down the silverware and rushed to greet our guests.

"The sitter cancelled," were the first words out of Josie's mouth. Christopher was tugging on her gold hoop earrings and she looked tired.

"It's fine," I said. "We can all entertain him." Josie looked apprehensive, as if not sure how to read my response. She knew how much I was looking forward to an all-adult evening. I adored Christopher, but I wanted Josie to get a break from him. She wouldn't hear of me taking him for a few hours so she could get her nails done, or something like that.

"Come in," I told them, holding open the screen door. "Jay's in the kitchen and I'll grab the toy basket from my closet." I sprinted up the steps and returned with the laundry basket full of trucks, blocks, and action figures that I kept on hand for just this kind of occasion.

I found everyone, including Jason, seated in the front room. The sofa barely accommodated three people, so Jason was sitting cross-legged on the floor. I crouched down next to him. "When will dinner be ready?" I whispered in his ear.

"Fifteen minutes, give or take," he told me, while getting to his feet. "May I get someone a glass of wine, beer, or some water?" The orders were given and my ever-gracious host returned to his domain to fix the drinks.

Tom sat silently, the TV remote in his hand. He had switched over to the baseball game and muted the sound. His feet were propped on the coffee table, one arm behind his head. Tom also appeared to be in his domain.

"Tom, a beer for you. Josie, you had water?" asked Jason. He held the tray casually with one hand, while handing out the orders. If I didn't know better, I would have thought he had worked as a waiter in his youth. Not Jason. No way. Jason worked as a file clerk at his father's law office as a kid. When I met him he was just getting started in real estate and was selling life insurance on the side. I'm sure he never even saw the inside of a bar until our wedding night.

"Yes, water. And I brought some special drinks for us ladies," she winked. "Paige, in the diaper bag, it's right there…can you reach? Yeah, that's it, the green pitcher, and there's two plastic margarita glasses in there, too." Josie shook the thermos and poured us each an icy drink.

"Of course you brought your own!" I laughed. She never ceased to amaze me. She brought her own coffee creamer to the diner last week, saying that she refused to drink those little creamers that have been frozen and then thawed and then frozen again. "It's just unhealthy, if you ask me," she had said.

Tonight, she was prepared. When I opened the bag, I saw she was also packing a bag of Tostitos and a jar of Pepe's hot salsa. "Never leave home without a pitcher of 'ritas. That's my motto. Isn't that like one of the things that the Army guys have to swear to or something? 'Always be prepared.'"

I shook my head and caught the look on Jason's face. It was something between confusion and distaste. I knew I would hear about it later. He thought Josie was a whacko. He just didn't *get* our relationship. He thought I should find a girlfriend that was more *like* me. I wondered if he really knew who I was.

"Hey Tom, how's the new job going?" I said, trying to pry his attention away from the TV for a minute. Josie rolled her eyes as if to say *don't bother.*

"Huh?" Tom responded, following this at once with "Hey, he's out, man! What the—?" And then he glanced toward me. "Sorry, my job?"

I leaned closer. "How are you liking it, the early shift?" Josie grabbed the remote and shoved it between the cushions of the couch.

Tom glared in her direction. "It's good and it beats the hell out of driving a truck all day."

"I'd hate to drive a truck," said Jason, and I loved that he was trying to find a way into the conversation. "It's bad enough that my clients keep me in my car all day. It's terrible for sciatica, all that pressure on the spine causing long-term damage. My acupuncturist says that many of her patients are drivers."

Tom nodded, as if he understood, but his eyes told us that he didn't give a hoot what my husband did all day, or understand why in the world anyone needed an acupuncturist. "I'd hate to drive around in your car all day, too, buddy," he replied, leaning over and punching Jason on the arm. Tom drove a pick-up truck, almost new, but functional. He was always teasing Jason about his basic-beige Buick, telling him it was an old man's car.

Jason ignored both the comment and the gesture and stood. "Time to bring out all the food. You go on into the dining room," he said, motioning toward the carefully set table. (After I had set it, he changed it all around, adding flowers, matching serving utensils, and candles. It was lovely, as always—almost as nice as going to a fancy restaurant.)

I followed him into the kitchen. "Can I bring something out for you?"

He was draining pasta in the colander. " I think I have it under control," he said, tipping the two-handled strainer until all the pasta had slipped onto the platter. "I hope everyone likes pasta," he added.

For a minute I thought he was pissed, but he turned and I saw that sweet smile of his. I put my arms around his neck. "Thanks for doing all this, honey."

Jason kissed the top of my head. My head fit just under his shoulder. It always felt like the safest place to be, when we first met.

I watched him organize the pasta in the decorative dish. "No problem," he said. "Maybe after dinner we can have an arm-wrestling contest. Or, hey, maybe we can see who can spit the farthest? What do you think?"

I scowled at him, he shrugged, and then swept past me, carrying the steaming bowl through the doorway. When he turned and winked at me, I smiled gratefully, grabbed the bread and wine and followed at his heels.

The dining room was small, just large for a table with six chairs, a buffet (that was actually a coffee table I'd covered with a decorative cloth), and a tall plant (fake, of course). Josie and I sat across from each other, Jason was at the head of the table, and Tom sat next to his wife. Christopher was happily hopping from one of the empty chairs to the other.

"Christopher, you little monkey, come here," Josie commanded. "I'm sorry," she said, looking straight at Jason.

Beads of sweat on Jason's forehead gave him away. And if that didn't, there was his straight back, or the way he lifted fork to mouth, which was set in one straight line. I saw that Josie was upset and wanted to rescue the evening.

"So, Paige tells me you've made some great sales this month."

Jason hated it when I told Josie anything about his life. "Whatever you two talk about," he had complained, "be sure it isn't me." He hated what he called "jibber jabber" between women and adamantly insisted that nothing about his life was Josie's business.

Jason's mouth did that pinching thing. "Well, yes," he said. "I've actually had two estate closings."

Josie looked at Jason for a moment, as if knowing that she wasn't getting anything else out of that topic. That's when she tried a new one. "The house is looking great. I wish our house were as put together as yours. Man, the work that still needs to be done in that shack is mind-boggling." She leaned her head on Tom's shoulder. "We love it, though."

"Yes, it really is a sound home," said Jason. "Good value there. The homes on this street are old, but they're still desired for their timeless architecture and solid construction. They don't build them like this anymore." He waved a finger back and forth, motioning ceiling to floor.

"You got that right, buddy," Tom piped in, chewing on the last of his pasta. "The house we had in Florida had paper-thin walls. I swear; one huge wind and the place would've been matchsticks."

Jason's eyes were slightly squinted and he pushed himself away from the table. "If you'll excuse me."

"Sure thing, boss," said Tom. "When nature calls, you gotta answer." He laughed, but it was a little too loud, like a combination of nerves and beer.

By the time dinner was finished, two bottles of Merlot were emptied and Jason and Tom argued one more time about global warming, Christopher, having chewed on his sliver of garlic bread until it was unrecognizable, began trying to clear the table.

Josie scooped Christopher from the highchair and handed him to Tom. "Can you take him home for his bath?" she asked. "I'll stay and help clean up." Tom hoisted the boy onto his chest. "Come on, big boy, let's get you to bed." He hiked the diaper bag over one shoulder. "Thanks, Jay. The food was great."

"Thank my mother," Jason said, smiling. "She thought we should all learn how to cook." Jason walked them to the door. "Hope the little guy goes to bed for you."

His tone reminded me of a Charlie Brown cartoon I saw years ago and how he heard his teacher's voice drone, "Wah, wah, wah, wah, wah," without any emotion or enthusiasm. When Jason spoke, it sounded scripted.

Tom smiled and said, "Isn't it about time you guys made a playmate for Chris?" As if cued, Christopher put his nose on Tom's shoulder and rubbed it into his shirt. "Bedtime," said Tom, offering one more thanks before leaving.

Jason was making his way into the kitchen when I headed him off. "You did all the work," I told him, "so we'll clean up." Josie was already clearing dishes from the table.

"You don't have to tell me twice," he said. "Just be careful with the dinnerware, okay?" He grabbed the latest copy of *Reader's Digest* and headed upstairs.

I watched him climb the stairs and wondered if he would ever recognize the qualities I so adored in my friends. But then I wondered if I cared. Maybe the answer was not to do these little gatherings, after which I always felt the need to apologize for his behavior.

I walked into the kitchen. When I was certain that Jason was upstairs,

I grabbed the dishcloth out of Josie's hand. "I went," I said to her, staring straight into her eyes, willing her to read my mind.

"You went where?" she asked.

I felt myself blushing. "To that doctor you told me about," I whispered. "I saw him today and he's sending me for some tests. After that, I guess Jay will have to go for tests, but I'm not sure yet. You didn't tell me he was a hundred years old, but I really liked him."

Josie laughed. "Yeah, he is ancient, isn't he? But I figure he's too old to really see what's down there, between my legs. In his case, they probably *do* look all alike to him, all furry and blurry!" Josie giggled, and I couldn't help laughing at the thought of that old doctor squinting at my private parts.

"Stop," I begged, taking a breath. "The doctor said I have to bring Jason next time, but what am I going to do? I never even told him I was going *this* time?" My fingers went directly to my mouth—a holdover of a nervous habit I had as a child—and I chewed on the sides of my fingers.

Josie grabbed the cloth back and began wiping down the granite counter. "It's inevitable, don't you think? It takes two people to have a baby. But you knew that, right?"

We finished cleaning the kitchen and I walked Josie to the door. I apologized for Jason's behavior. "Sometimes," I said, "I want to scream. Tell Tom that he means well, but he's just so—"

Josie cut me off. "Stop apologizing, okay? It is what it is." She put her hand on my shoulder and my eyes starting to fill with tears.

"I'll call you in the morning," said Josie. She was thinking of looking for more wallpaper and asked me to tag along. "You're so much better at that color-coordinating junk, anyway," she said, looking at the newly painted walls in the entrance.

"Sure, call me," I said.

Josie took a few steps away and then turned back. "Get him to go, Paige. You have to start sometime."

I stood there, watching my friend cross the street. I saw the dim light coming from Christopher's room and felt a familiar pang of envy. Closing the door, I headed up the stairs. It was now or never.

Six

"Friendship improves happiness, and abates misery, by doubling our joys, and dividing our grief."
—Anonymous

The steady squeak of the wooden rocker on Josie's front porch created a rhythm that almost lulled me to sleep. Fall was coming again; the leaves on the big maples in front of her house were tinged with gold. Halloween witches and goblins lined the walkways of several homes along the street. Fluorescent figures were stuck in the ground so the candy-seeking children could find the front doors, and pumpkins carefully carved into unique scary faces were showing up on front stoops and porches.

"Hi, stranger!" came Josie's voice, the metal screen door banging shut behind her. "That damn door," she muttered. "I hope it didn't wake Christopher." She put her ear to the screen. Giving a satisfied nod, she scooted past me.

"Did he just go down?" I asked, watching my friend settle onto the porch swing. The chains were rusted and the seat splintered, but it was her favorite place to sit. Curled up, legs under and her hair tucked into a baseball cap, she looked about eleven. Her face was clean and shiny and her overalls were a little too big, which only added to the child-like appearance. If I'd had my camera, it would have been the perfect photograph. This was Josie in her element.

"He had a busy morning, and was up most of the night cutting more teeth. I'll be glad when these molars come in." Josie leaned forward and gave the swing a gentle push.

It was a glorious day, my favorite time of year. Not too hot and not too cold. "So," I asked, stretching my legs. "What does Tom think of the plum walls?" Josie had gone out on a limb with that color, knowing that Tom hated dark-colored rooms. Nevertheless, she had still chosen a deeply muted plum for the walls. It was absolutely stunning with the sage accents and gold picture frames. Her decorating proved to be much keener than mine. Thankfully, she followed her own advice.

"He doesn't care," laughed Josie, "as long as he doesn't have to do it." She scooted the other rocker closer to mine. "You want something to drink? I got coffee and water, that's about it."

I was still full from lunch. It was my thirty-sixth birthday and Jason had taken me to my favorite restaurant. When I looked in the mirror that morning, I saw a thirty-six year-old woman, but in my heart I felt so much younger, closer to twenty-six. It was as if I had lost time somewhere. For example, I remember my first apartment as if it were yesterday, not eighteen years ago. It was in a damp basement in an old woman's home, close to the technical college where I was taking cosmetology. The carpet was green shag and the walls paneled with dark walnut plank, giving the place a cave-like feel. There was a galley-style kitchen with wallpapered kitchen cabinets, a tiny bath, and a living area that doubled as a bedroom, with its sleeper sofa. It made me smile, remembering the firemen breaking through the window after I left a grilled cheese sandwich on the stove and hopped in the shower. My culinary talents hadn't improved much since those days, but I had learned how to make a sandwich without burning the house down. Jason would not be amused by that story, nor by many others that I kept tucked away in my "those were the days" files.

"Happy birthday!" announced Josie. She stuck her hand into her pocket and pulled out a small package. It was neatly wrapped in foil gift paper, the kind that came from specialty stores.

I loved presents, especially those I received from Josie. She had this uncanny ability to come up with ideas that blew me away. The first year, when I turned thirty-four, I found a paper bag on my doorstep. It was filled with paper clips attached into a chain. On the bottom of the bag were toast crumbs and sugar. The card read:

> *To My Dearest and Most Neurotic Friend, Paige,*
> *May toast crumbs never fall at your feet,*
> *Nor sugar spill for you to sweep.*
> *May your paper clips be ever neat*
> *And God help us if these three do meet.*

I had laughed hysterically at the gift: paper clips, toast crumbs and spilled sugar were my three biggest peeves.

I turned my attention back to the package and tried to imagine what clever gift she had come up with this year. I shook the package; it didn't rattle. My heart started to beat a little faster. Peeling back the paper, I discovered another layer, only this was the kind used in brown paper sacks. With my anticipation growing, I opened the box and peered inside. There was an odd-looking metal ring, a band decorated with six knots. Set into one knot was a cobalt blue gemstone, its color unlike any I had ever seen. It was translucent, but dark, the gold flecks in the stone catching the sunlight. Attached to the band was a tag that read:

The Ring of Fertility: This six-knotted ring is an ancient symbol for fertility. Enhanced with the brilliant Lapis Lazuli, the love-drawing stone dedicated to the goddesses Aphrodite, Venus, and Iris. It was thought to keep the body healthy and the soul free from error, envy, or fear. It is most loved, and worn as, a fertility stone.

Tears sprang to my eyes. I reached over and squeezed Josie close to me. "Perfect, as always," I told her. "God, Jo, how do you do it?" I marveled at the ring, now on my finger. "And it's a perfect fit."

"I found it online, while I was searching for infertility info. You're supposed to turn it three times before you do the nasty, and it's supposed to increase your chances of getting pregnant—or so they say. You know," she added. "What's really cool is that it's also considered the stone of friendship and truth."

"I love it!"

Josie smiled broadly. "I'm so glad!" After a moment, she asked how my appointment had gone.

Back to reality: the gift was fun, but it was unlikely to cure my baby problems, and Jason was still denying there was a problem, insisting instead that we were trying too hard.

"It went fine," I told her. "I had the ultrasound, some blood work, and some dye test to see if anything's blocked. Now I have to wait for the results." When Josie nodded, I decided to tell her more. "Jay changes the subject every time I bring it up. I've tried to tell him, but he says he's too tired to go through it again. He knows about the tests, but that's it. He wasn't even surprised that I had gone to the doctor."

I stood up and started to pace back and forth, staring at my feet, while Josie waited for me to go on. "I guess he thinks it's my problem. I don't know, it was weird." I leaned against the railing and stared across the road. After a moment, I finally said what was on my mind. "Josie, I'm beginning to wonder if he even wants kids."

Josie leaned back and grabbed the wiry limb of the tree that was resting on the edge of the porch, pulled it toward her and then let it go. "You guys talked about kids before you got married, right? So what's the deal with him?" She leaned across the porch railing to retrieve the branch.

"Beats me. It's like, the more I talk about it, the less interested he is. It is so frustrating, especially when I see all these couples at that clinic who are so 'into' the process…and then there's us?"

I stared off into the distance and reflected on my life, my choices, and what it was that guided my future. Two thoughts ran through my head: *I wish I knew the answer* and *I wish it were easy.*

"I know the way Jason's mind works," I told her. "He figures that it's best for me to get all these tests done and *then* we'll sit down with the doctor and figure out what's wrong. Since it's all my problem, why should he have to go and blah, blah, blah." I stood and paced the porch again, sliding my hand along the wooden rail and picking up a few slivers along the way.

"So when will you know?" Josie asked.

I picked the slivers from my hand. "Probably by next Tuesday, so it's not that long. It wasn't bad, the tests, and I really didn't need Jason there, but still—" I felt myself starting to crumble again. "It's just that—" Josie came over and wrapped her arms around me.

"Whatever you need, I'm here." She leaned back and looked me in the eye. "This can't be easy, going through it on your own. He'll come around, Paige, he's just running scared."

I knew that Josie was trying to reassure me, but I wasn't so easily reassured. Nor was I sure that, after all those years of marriage, Jason might not be content without children. "Whenever I talk, he puts me off. It's so infuriating, sometimes I'm tempted to give up."

Just then, I saw a minivan pull into my driveway. "It's Mr. Harris and the gang," I said, pointing toward the elderly people coming from the retirement home. "It's cute. They come every month for a haircut, the three of them. I guess they're about eighty years old, each of them. I hope I'm as spry when I'm their age. I couldn't handle being a burden on anyone. You know?"

Josie nodded vigorously. "When it's my time to go, I just hope it's quick, like getting run over by a train. Done. No lingering, and I'll be damned if anyone is going to change my diapers or feed me with a spoon. Not that Tom wouldn't," she added, her voice softer. "'Cause I know he would. But I wouldn't do that to him. I just couldn't. You're my witness. Pull the plug, Paige! No life support!" She shouted after me. Mr. Harris turned to the sound just as I was coming up behind him. I guided them toward the back door, turning to shake my head at Josie. She was smiling.

***

I was soaking in a hot tub filled with the Zen healing bubbles I had bought myself when Jason knocked on the bathroom door. "Come on in, hon, I'm in my birthday suit."

He looked somber, as if he had seen a ghost.

"Paige, we have to talk." His forehead wrinkled when he spoke, which usually meant he was worried.

I pulled myself to a sitting position amid the mass of bubbles and propped both elbows on the tub's rim. "Right now? Can't it wait?"

He shook his head and sat on the lid of the toilet. "I don't want you…it's just that…" Jason was not one for being at a loss for words.

"Jason, what?" I asked. "You're scaring me." I tried to read his eyes, but there was something unfamiliar about them.

"I've been thinking a lot about this baby stuff," he started.

"You and me both, but why are you bringing this up today? When I tried to talk to you about it this morning, you pushed it away." I often wondered if all marriages were like this, a constant shuffle between love and hate. That day, on my birthday, he suddenly wanted to talk.

Jason grabbed a towel off the rack and handed it to me. "I'll be in the bedroom."

My heart was pounding, but I wasn't sure if I was nervous or just so angry that my husband would drag me out of the tub to *talk*, when all I had tried to do for the last three months was discuss our future plans. I dried off, climbed into my warm pajamas, and hurried into the next room, where I found Jason sitting on the bed. He was leaning against the wooden headboard, his arms folded behind his head. Wanting to make eye contact, I took a seat on the chair across from the bed.

"You have my attention," I said. "What is it?" When he said nothing, I felt my body get stiff. "Jason, I've been trying to get you to talk about this forever, and *now* you decide it's time, and that I'm just supposed to stop and listen. Is that it?" My face felt flush; the veins in my temples started to pulse. "So talk!" I was not a yeller, but these months of frustration were arriving in one mammoth wave.

Jason took a deep breath. "You don't have to get hostile, Paige. I don't like that tone you're using."

I jumped to my feet. "I don't give a shit what tone I'm using!" I nearly screamed. "And I don't give a rat's ass if you don't like me yelling!" My voice crackled, unused to the volume.

Jason clucked like a hen. "I knew that she'd rub off on you one day. Listen to yourself. You're better than that, Paige. Using that foul language doesn't look good on you, dear. What would our friends think of you if they heard you cursing like a damn truck driver? It's disgraceful."

I stood there watching him, his head shaking back and forth, and an image from the past darted through my mind. My father often shook his head when I displeased him. And no matter how hard I tried to please him, it was never enough. I never chose the right friends; my clothes were all wrong. "Girls who wear clothes like that are looking for trouble. Are you looking for trouble, Paige?" he would ask me. "Well, girly, you're sure to find it wearing that getup. Why not just put a sign around your neck that tells everyone you're a whore? Is that what you want people to think?"

I remember bowing my head in shame for disappointing him and then quickly changing into something more appropriate for a young lady.

The sound of water running out of the tub brought me out of the daydream. Jason was standing tall in front of me, and my heart felt as if it were on fire. "Things were great with us before she moved in. She puts all these ideas in your head. Can't you see that she's just not, well, she's not good for you? She's changed you and I disapprove of your relationship with her, Paige. I really don't think it's healthy."

I listened; my temples throbbed. "STOP! Who are you talking about? Do you mean my best friend Josie? She has a name, you know, and she's a hell of a lot more of a presence in my life these days than you are…dear!" It felt good to mimic the condescending tone he used it with me whenever he was disapproving. "And by the way, please don't bring anyone else into this. You're the one who wanted to talk, so talk, damn it!"

He shook his head at me, slowly. "If you'd stop yelling."

What a condescending asshole. "Go ahead, here's your moment. Use it."

Jason took a book off the nightstand, one of the books I had asked him to read. It was about fertility problems, with options for people who couldn't conceive. I didn't even know he had looked at it. He pointed to the cover. "After lunch, all I could think about was this baby stuff."

I relaxed my shoulders. "Is that what it is to you, 'baby stuff'? Jason, we talked about this before we were married. We wanted children, didn't we? So why are you so against finding out the problem??"

"You would have known what I'm feeling, if you had come home after lunch, instead of traipsing over to her house." He gestured toward the window. "I had no chance to react to what you were saying earlier."

I wanted to hit him; he was so full of it. How dare he put this on me. I wanted to slap his face. "No chance to react, Jason? How about when I asked you, 'Jason, are you sure you want to have kids?' Did you have any response when we talked last month, last week, last night—this morning? So don't give me that shit. It's just always on your terms!" I was yelling again, and my head felt like a truck had rumbled through it.

"If you're going to continue shouting at me, we aren't going to get anywhere. I'm sorry. I'm sorry I didn't respond when you wanted me to; I'm sorry I haven't wanted talk about this. I'm sorry."

He did look sorry, for a moment, but what was he really sorry for?

I was afraid to ask again, but I had to. "Jason, do you want children?"

The hesitation gave it away. Oh, my God. After all those years of trying, he didn't even want children? I was losing it; my hands began to shake. "Answer me!"

When he turned toward me, I caught a tear in his eye. Just one, but it was there.

"I don't know," he said.

I never imagined that three quiet words could change my life—our life, together. Hot tears instantly sprang to my eyes and began to trickle slowly down my cheeks. I felt as though I had just been punched in the gut. I lowered myself onto the corner of the bed, stretched out my hands behind me to steady myself. He kept talking. I could see his lips moving but his voice sounded distant.

"I need time to think, Paige. There are things I need to work out. I can't do it here." He opened the closet and pulled down an overnight bag.

It was as if a fist had closed around my heart. First the man I love tells me he may not want children, now he's leaving me. Any thoughts of a birthday quickly disappeared.

I tried to speak, but my mouth turned dry and the words stuck in my throat. I finally managed, "You're leaving me?" A tear fell from my chin and splashed against my knee.

"Paige, don't go crazy on me. Of course I'm not *leaving* you."

I sucked in air, trying to fill my lungs, which suddenly felt empty. "Today, on my birthday? You're leaving me?"

Jason's shoulders suddenly dropped and I saw the anger run out of him.

"I need time alone to think," he said. "Just a few days away, that's all. Can you at least give me that?"

My eyes were burning and my chest was on fire. I picked up the book on fertility and threw it at him. "Get the fuck out!"

I watched him turn slowly away from me and retrieve his overnight bag, and then, just as slowly, he walked out of the bedroom.

Seven

"Friendship is certainly the finest balm for the pangs of disappointed love"
—Jane Austen

"Yes, two o'clock this afternoon—pardon me? Your husband? Hmmm. I didn't have him on the schedule, but bring him along and I'll squeeze him in." I thanked the woman, hung up, and turned to find Josie's face pressed against the glass of the front door. I waved her in with one hand, rubbed my temple with the other. Nothing seemed to help the pain.

I glanced in the mirror. My hair was a disaster, swept up in a quick ponytail that was half to one side, with wisps of hair flying this way and that. I was wearing sweat pants—the ugly ones, with an elastic cuff on the bottom and a bleach stain on the knee, left over from cleaning the tub—and a tie-dyed T-shirt.

"Hiya chick, how's it going?" Josie put Christopher on the floor and reached for her coffee mug. "Busy day?"

I smiled and brushed my hair off my face. "I'm swamped. Thursdays are starting to be *the* day for hair in this neighborhood. Am I missing out on something? Mrs. Peterson rescheduled from tomorrow to this morning, so I don't have time to do my own hair today. Then, the twins are coming in again for a set and I have a color at noon. Mrs. McFann is finally getting rid of the pink hair she desperately had to have last year."

Josie stared at me as I rambled on and then poured me a fresh cup of coffee and placed it in front of me. After all this time, she knew me, knew that my babbling about nothing usually meant I was avoiding talking about *something*. She settled into her favorite chair and wrapped her hand around the hot mug. "And so you—"

I felt tears forming at the back of my throat. "Jason left me," I blurted out. "He's gone, Josie."

"What do you mean, gone? He can't be gone." She looked around the kitchen, as if he would be standing there.

I felt my jaw tighten. "He said he needed time to think," I told her, hearing anger in my voice. "He left last night…to think. Some birthday present, huh? Stupid me, I always said he never surprised me on my birthday. Well, let me tell you, this year he wins the birthday surprise contest." I shook my head, as if trying to shake off the reality of this abandonment.

Josie didn't look nearly as devastated as I felt. "Uh-huh," she said. "So he needed some time, big deal. He'll be back." She studied the mug and took a drink. "Guys are such babies. Did he say where he was going?"

Her voice pressed me, the way it always did when Josie wanted the facts. She wasn't one for emotions. She once told me that she had never been introspective and found it easiest to ignore her emotions, rather than deal with them. Now that I knew her better, I didn't believe a word of that. She was as emotional as I was, but did a better job of keeping it all balanced. Or keeping it all hidden, I wasn't quite sure. Me, I'm the freak-out queen and *emotional discretion* is not in my vocabulary. I've always worn my emotions like a dangling bracelet on my arm. The problem is that they're always exposed, easily damaged. As they were on the day after Jason walked out.

"How the hell should I know where he's going?" I snapped. "One minute I'm enjoying a quiet bubble bath, the next minute my life is spiraling out of control. He said he wasn't sure about having a baby and needed time alone to think about it." I gulped the coffee, wanting to feel the caffeine swimming through my veins, like an alcoholic craves the rush of that first drink. My temple pulsed to the beat of my heart and I became temporarily mesmerized by the rhythm.

Josie smiled and snapped her fingers near my face. When I looked at her, she said, "Okay, let's think for a minute. There's got to be something way worse than this."

I thought she was losing her mind. My life was shit; my husband just left me, and I couldn't get pregnant. What could be worse than that? Josie smiled, as if reading my mind. "When I was growing up, my older brother played this game with me: when I was upset, he'd tell me to think of something worse and I was supposed to come up with something that was even more horrible than not having a date to the Spring Fling. It always made me feel better. It can't hurt to try."

A reluctant smile crept across my face. "Think of something worse, huh? Okay, it would be worse if I didn't have legs, 'cause then I couldn't kick my husband's ass!" I found myself laughing at the image, but it didn't last. "Seriously, I can't think of anything worse than this. Everything feels like it's crashing down around me; I can't think straight."

"I know, sweetie." She patted my hand. "He'll be back in a day or two, maybe not even that long—he's just messed up, too. He needs to coddle his male ego, do some serious soul-searching, and figure out what he really wants. It won't take long. He just needs to do it his way, for now."

I gave her a questioning look. This wasn't like her. I expected her to tell me what an ass he was being, how stupid he was and how I was better off without him. Why was it I felt like such a failure?

Josie leaned on the table, resting her head on her hand. "He loves you, Paige. He's probably scared that he can't give you what you want the most. I'll bet that's why he doesn't go for those damned tests. He's afraid it's really him. God help me, if he finds out it's his swimmers that aren't making it to the pool, you won't be able to live with him anyway."

I sat back in the chair, absorbing some of what Josie was saying. It wasn't about me. It *was* really about him. "You know what, you're right. Jay was always a runner. I mean, he hates confrontation and he knows this is a *biggie*. He'll stew for a bit and then he'll talk. I never really thought about how he was feeling." Suddenly, I wasn't feeling so angry. "I was so upset with him for not listening that I assumed he was ignoring me, or worse—blaming me for everything," I looked imploringly at my friend. "God, I am so confused; I feel like I'm rowing with one oar, and I'm getting really tired."

Josie nodded and put her arm around my shoulder. "So as dumb as he was for springing this on you, maybe the break will do you both some good." She stood up. "Tom's home early tonight, so what do ya say we hit Panchos for a margarita and some chips?" Without waiting for me to respond, she announced, "I'll come by around eight!"

I looked at the clock. "I'm doing a perm at four so, yeah, she should be done by six. Sure, that sounds good, but I have to be back by ten."

Josie shook her head. "My Paige, always the party animal! Fine, I promise to get you home by ten." She held up her coffee cup. "Can I take this to go? I have a ton of running around to do." I poured her fresh cup into Jason's new travel mug—the bastard would just have to travel without it.

"Be ready at eight and don't dress up," Josie said. "But you might want to lose the sweats." I looked down at the pilled blue track pants and nodded. I still had time to change before my client arrived with her famous double-decker brownies.

***

I was always curious to know more about Josie's past. She was a great conversationalist, but she rarely talked about her past. I knew that her brother died and that her parents were also gone. I also knew she had a sister, Judith. I'd met her a few times and couldn't stand her. Judith was one of those stuck-up, single women who wore designer clothes, drove expensive cars, and looked at you, her face a half smile, half smirk. She even admitted to playing golf because she loved wearing the skirt and hanging out at the clubhouse with the guys.

I held the teacup with both hands, blowing into it. "More importantly," I asked, "what have you scratched *off* the list?"

"In my lifetime? Hmm, I learned how to drive, I had sex in an elevator, skinny-dipped in a hot tub along with six other people, had my belly button pierced, spent a week on a fishing boat, backpacked in Mexico, had a child—nothing too exciting." She smiled.

Nothing too exciting! "Josie, are you out of your mind? Sex in public, skinny-dipping, and body piercing? I think the riskiest thing I ever did was go to the grocery store without makeup!" I was so drawn to her adventurous side and I was fascinated by how confident she was about things that absolutely terrified me. That fascination scared the hell out of Jason. He was probably worried I'd join a cult, pierce my nipples, or get a tattoo of a rattlesnake on my ass if I hung around with Josie. The truth is, she was so much more vulnerable than anyone knew, except me.

It took a moment for me to realize that Josie was speaking.

"Paige, you have to take risks," she said, hands waving through the air. "Life is for living, girl! You can't go around picking up all the bruised apples at the bottom of the tree, know what I mean? You have to fill your basket with ripe ones. They always taste better when you pick them yourself, anyway."

What was this, her new philosophy? I smiled because I understood what she was saying: take a risk, dare to stick out my neck. Josie was always trying to get me to join her on one of her little adventures, but I always had an excuse.

Even when Josie joined that yoga class, it symbolized something to me. Not that yoga can be compared to bungee jumping, but it was one more way that my friend tasted life. She didn't just bite into it, she savored every aspect of it. I wanted to taste it, too, but I was always afraid of failing, of looking like an idiot. What if I couldn't do it? What would that say about me?

Eight

"Life is like music; it must be composed by ear, feeling, and instinct, not by rule."

—Samuel Butler

I arrived home to find the light on the answering machine blinking. I felt an overwhelming panic mixed with fear. It had to be Jason, but what he was calling to tell me? That he had decided to never come home? What if he really didn't want kids? What if it was the end of everything I thought my life was about? Hesitantly, I clicked the button on the machine. Without so much as a pause, his sexy voice was filling the living room. "Hi. I guess you're out. Well, I really want to talk to you, so can you call me at Jim's? I'll be up for a while." There was a delay, where all I could hear was static—like the quiet hum you hear when you put a seashell to your ear—and then "Paige, I love you. I'm sorry. Call me, okay?"

Call me. That's what he wanted me to do. Call him? I felt resentment building and wasn't sure it was the right time to talk. *Call me.* All these months I had tried to get him to make some decisions about our future, and it came down to this.

Picking up the receiver, I dialed the number. Jim was Jason's twin brother. He lived thirty minutes away, in Des Moines. Jason wanted to live closer to the big city, but we couldn't afford to when we decided to buy a house. I, on the other hand, had no desire to live anywhere but here. The quiet, family-oriented neighborhoods of Maple Grove, the tree-lined streets and small-town atmosphere—this was my kind of place.

Yet another thing on which we disagreed.

His brother answered the phone. "Jim, is Jason still up?"

"Hi, Paige, hang on a sec," he said, and then hollered, "Hey Jay, you up? Phone's for you."

I heard the rustle, a hand going over the receiver, a click, and then my husband's voice.

"Sorry," he said. "I wanted to get the cordless. The kids are watching the game." He hesitated, as though waiting for me to start. Since I was the one who always started, over and over, I decided that it was his turn. "So," he went on. "I called because I wanted to talk. Is this a good time?"

I hesitated. "Yeah, it's fine, I'm listening." I took a deep breath, trying hard to relax my clenched shoulders. I heard Jason clear his throat and dreaded what he was about to say. My stomach lurched.

"First of all," he said, "I'm sorry I left so suddenly. That was not the answer, and I knew it the minute I left. It's just that you were in the tub and I started rifling through all those papers and saw pages and pages of that clinical stuff—*male infertility; what to do when you're sterile; conception solutions*—and I panicked. I know that sounds cowardly, but...Paige, it suddenly became real to me and I felt like I was suffocating."

I sat there trying to absorb what he had said. I recognized the real fear in his voice and my heart softened. "What part of it became real?" The man was really in pain about this. How long had he been holding it in and why the hell hadn't he talked to me about it?

"I don't know how to explain it, without sounding like an absolute jerk," he said. "At first, it was kind of fun, having sex so much. What man would complain about that?"

I smiled, remembering how he had joked about it being "baby-making time." I'd forgotten how interested he was, in the beginning. Was I so wrapped up in my own self-pity that I had missed the signs of my husband's misery over our failure to conceive a child?

"But then it got to be tedious," he went on. "You started getting more and more stressed every month, and I started to back off. It wasn't intentional, but I know I disconnected from the whole thing a long time ago. I saw it eating away at you and figured if I let it go, it might go away. You talked about it, Paige, but I pretended it didn't exist, and then I justified it by telling myself that it would happen…when the time was right." He let out a huge sigh.

"Jason, I didn't know how you were feeling, you should've told me," I said. "Can we talk about this at home?" I wanted him home; I wanted him close to me. My body ached to be held, to be comforted in his arms.

"I'll be right home."

***

"All right, I've waited long enough, now tell me what happened or I'll scream!" Josie exclaimed as we rounded the corner of the frozen foods section at Murray's Grocer. "Put that box of croutons down and tell me why I see a familiar car in your driveway?" Josie tugged the box out of my hands and set it on the shelf next to the soda biscuits.

I grinned sheepishly. "Well, when I got home last night, I found a message from Jay. He was at his brother's place, but then he came home. That's it." I retrieved the croutons and tossed the box into my cart.

I turned to see Josie giving Christopher a handful of animal crackers. Then she grabbed the side of my cart. "Look, lady, I want all the details. Are you having a baby? Does he want a baby? Did you have great makeup sex? That is the best, isn't it?" Her grin made me laugh.

I leaned on the cart. "Let's see," I said, ticking each response off. "Yes, he wants a baby. And yes, the makeup sex was incredible." I smiled, my eyes filling with tears. "He's coming with me next week to see the doctor."

"Yippee!" she hollered, jumping up and down. Shoppers were stopping in the aisles to see who was yelling. "Oh, I'm so happy he came to his senses…finally!" She moved closer and asked, "Did you kick his sorry ass for leaving you on your birthday?"

"I wouldn't say I kicked his ass, but I did rough him up a bit. I gave him a bit of a workout, if you know what I mean." I felt my cheeks heat up. Pushing the cart around a display of cereal, I headed toward the checkout.

"You go, girl!" said Josie, right behind me. "I'm glad you two kissed and made up. So it's next Tuesday, right?"

"To get the test results? Yes, Tuesday. Why?"

"I go for my yearly checkup on Wednesday, so I was hoping you could watch Christopher for me."

I told her I'd be delighted. "Do you think we could get frequent-flyer miles for these medical visits? I've been to see the doctor a few times, and now you. He should at least offer a free pap smear for the referral."

Josie laughed. "I can see the ad now: *Spread your legs for us and your referring friend will get a free sample of our new PMS formula.*"

I was holding my stomach from laughing so hard. "Stop!" I gasped. "I'm gonna pee!" I tried to catch my breath and the cashier looked at us like we were lunatics. Josie just kept pointing at me and shrugging and the cashier nodded, which made me laugh even more. By the time I got to the car with my three bags of groceries, I was worn out.

"It's good to see you laugh again," Josie said. "And I'll definitely be thinking of you when I'm in those stirrups. Maybe I *will* ask the old guy for a discount. You are a frequent visitor, after all, and he only gets me once a year." She strapped Christopher into his car seat and I loaded our groceries into her van. The roads were clear, too early for weekend traffic. All the commuters would be filling the highways after two o'clock and I was glad that Jason didn't have to travel the freeway to get home from the office. Those drivers were crazy. In truth, I was even more relieved that I didn't have to drive. It's not that I couldn't, it's that I hated to, especially in traffic. Driving was one of those things on my "fears" list. Josie was the polar opposite: she loved to drive. In fact, she loved getting up on Sunday mornings, before daylight, and driving the country roads, just to breathe in the air. She said it was the most peaceful time of her week. I loved her description of the vibrant colors of the sky as the sun peeked over the horizon. She described the quiet rustle of cornfields, with the early morning breeze blowing through the crops. She once told me that this was the closest thing to heaven she could imagine.

The light turned green and Josie pulled out of the parking lot and onto Elm Street. I waved at Mrs. Peterson, who was walking her toy poodle. I also noticed that the mailman had been by, because all the flags were down on the rows of mailboxes. It was a beautiful fall day.

"I have to ask," Josie said, breaking the silence as she pulled into her driveway. "Did you tell Jason everything?" Josie knew about the rape, but it was all she knew. I couldn't bear to tell her that I had given away my baby, had turned away from possibly my one chance to have a child. And I certainly couldn't tell her that I had given my daughter to strangers. Josie knew practically everything about me, but not this. There are some secrets we have to keep.

I leaned my head against the headrest. "I'll tell him, Josie, I have to." How could I tell Jason about the rape? I had never told anyone, until Josie. But it was different with her. She had this way of dragging things out of me, things I didn't even know I cared about sharing. I'm not sure if she read it in my eyes or if just caught me when I was feeling entirely sorry for myself. Whatever it was, she got it out of me.

But not the baby, there was no telling her about that. I'd gone over the scenario more than once, imagining how she would react, and each time it ended with her thinking of me differently. I couldn't take a chance of that happening.

If I had been honest then, I would have understood that Josie's response would have been sympathetic; she would have understood. Not like my father. I remember the cold look he gave me when he found out; I can still see that disgust in his eyes. And it never left, from that day forward, even after I moved out at the age of seventeen. At the time, I told myself that I couldn't take it if Josie looked at me with those eyes, that I would die.

I realized that Josie was speaking and turned toward her.

"He might be mad that you waited all these years," she said quietly. "You know, and never told him about it." Josie scooped a sleeping Christopher into her arms. "Whatever you do, don't tell him that I know anything about it, okay?"

Josie was right; I couldn't let Jason know that Josie had known first.

He would be hurt, and rightly so. He joked that Josie and I were married and made light of our relationship when he wanted to cut deep. I knew even then that he was jealous.

"Never," I said, shaking my head. "But he'll probably figure it out, since he knows I tell you everything."

Well, almost everything.

Nine

"No passion so effectually robs the mind of all its powers of acting and reasoning as fear."
—Edmund Burke

When I was a child, I played with dolls. I didn't play baseball, take gymnastics lessons, or try out for cheerleading or swim team. My mother told me I was too delicate for sports, so I didn't bother trying out with my friends for any sports. Besides, there was never any time. As an only child in a family where my father was often away on business, I spent many hours with my mother, which is probably why I was so domesticated at such an early age. She enjoyed my company and was nervous about being alone in the house. I watched her take care of it all—house, money, bills, doctor's appointments, everything—and she told me that being a good wife meant always thinking ahead.

"Always have a nice dinner waiting, and be sure you're all fixed up when he comes home," she told me. "No man wants to come home to find his wife looking a mess."

My mother never looked a mess. Not from the outside.

There wasn't much time for fun when I was little, so I made up an imaginary family. My Mrs. Bentley doll was the mother. She had black-rimmed glasses and wore a white apron over her polka-dotted body suit. To me, she looked very maternal. My Softee Baby filled in as the youngest child. I gave her a brother when I found a Ken doll, with only one leg, in the parking lot of a K-Mart. I was glad she had a brother; it would've been nice if I had one…a real one. Every day, when my mother was busy fussing with some household task, I set up my make-believe family. Sometimes they picnicked in our big backyard, under the hot summer sun; other times, when it was snowy and cold, they enjoyed a sleigh ride down the sidewalks near our house. The neighbors always smiled as I passed by with my family of friends.

I wish I could've made that one-legged Ken doll come to life that day in October, when the new neighbor came over looking for a cup of milk. Mom had just left for her weekly errands and I was told not to let anyone in. I was sure she meant people I didn't know, and I knew the man next door. He had moved in the month before, when the neighbors relocated to Wisconsin. I had seen my mom talking to him, asking him if he wouldn't mind mowing the lawn once in a while. She told me he was a nice young man, so when he knocked, I opened the door.

***

I heard Jason call me from upstairs, his voice squeaky. He always squeaked when he was nervous, although he would never admit it.

"Have you seen my blue tie?" he called down.

"In the laundry basket!" I shouted. Today was The Day, our appointment with Dr. Peterson to go over the test results. My stomach did a back flip and the muffin I had just finished landed in my gut with a thud. It was the same sick feeling I had the night before, when I finally broached the subject that had plagued my every waking thought for years.

After pouring Jason a glass of his favorite Chablis, I carried it in to him and settled next to him in the living room. I dimmed the lights a little, too, so he couldn't see the fear in my face.

"I have to talk to you about something," I said, knowing how he hated conversations that started that way. How else could I begin? "It's about something that happened to me a long time ago."

He shifted, turning more toward me, and I could see that my statement intrigued him. "You make it sound so ominous," he said.

Why did this frighten me so much? It wasn't like I did anything wrong. I filled my lungs with air and slowly exhaled. "A long, long time ago, when I was a teenager, I was raped. I'm sorry I never told you." There, it was out. I searched his face in the dim light for something, anything that would lead me to know how, or if, to tell him the rest. I felt the tears begin to well in my eyes. The word "rape" stung my tongue and I felt suddenly nauseated. I tried to breathe deeply, each breath catching on the air as if it were murky water.

Jason moved to me, put his arms around me, and stroked my hair. "Don't cry, honey, it's okay; it's okay."

I pulled away. "It's not okay, Jason. I wish it were, but it's not. And it hasn't been okay since the moment that monster put his hands on me. He changed everything." A chill ran through my body and I cried out, "There's more! There's more and I'm afraid to tell you."

He pulled back, as if a defense mechanism had kicked in. "You're afraid?" he said. "That's nice to know." He returned to the couch. "If it's too difficult to talk about, that's one thing, and I can understand. I mean, I won't understand how you feel, but I can try." He hesitated and then admitted, "I don't know what I mean."

I could tell he was stumbling for the right thing to say and I certainly didn't blame him for being caught off guard. On his own, Jason was as insecure about how to answer tough questions as I was. The difference was, he didn't like to admit it.

I took a very deep breath and tried not to think that the future of my marriage rested on what I was about to say. "There's more, Jason, much more." I told myself to spit it out! Since the day I had delivered my baby, she was never mentioned again. Life went on for everyone, including me, and we pretended she never existed. Until I wrote it on that information form, I had deleted her from my history.

Or had I? All those years when I went for my yearly checkups, not once did I acknowledge that I had ever been pregnant. Why now?

I cleared my throat. I felt Jason's eyes burning into the side of my face and I gathered my courage and turned back to him. "There was—a baby." I stared at him, waiting for something, anything. I wanted him to scream in disbelief, get angry, walk away, I didn't care. But he gave me only silence. I didn't know what to do with that. I had lived with a quiet murmur behind closed doors, where my parents held our secret close at heart, ever fearful of its release. I endured the not-so-subtle distaste in my father's eyes, as if my very existence reminded him that he had failed to protect me from the evil lurking in the outside world. As I grew older, he spent more time away and the house became increasingly silent, until I finally left home.

Silence—I didn't need it now; I needed something much more real, something I could feel. The pain began to resurface, as if years of anesthesia were finally wearing off, in that silence of my own living room. And I wanted desperately to feel.

"Say something!" I heard myself yell, and Jason blinked back a tear rolling down his cheek. "And don't say you're sorry, please. I was raped, I had a baby, and now she's gone."

"When?" His voice shaky. "When?"

I lowered my head, accustomed to the shame I had felt growing up with this secret hidden in my soul. I felt it fighting to find a voice. "I had a little girl," I told him. "I was fifteen when she was born, Jay, fifteen. She was so beautiful, so tiny. If only you could have seen her." I shook my head. "I didn't want you to know about it. I don't know why, but I was so ashamed. And I gave her up, Jay; I gave her away. I gave up my own baby."

My body began to shake violently, hot tears burning into my cheeks. I don't know how long he let me cry, but it felt good to release the pain. When I was spent, my heart felt as if it had swelled inside my chest. It was a physical pain and it felt wonderfully real.

"I don't know if—" I said, but stopped. I needed a breath. "I'm so afraid that, after all this time, I'm being punished for it." Jason came to me and cradled me in his arms, his strong body covering me, warming me. We stayed like that for a long while, rocking together in a steady rhythm. It had been too long since I had felt so safe with him. In that moment, all my fears were swept away and I knew that, in the end, it would be all right.

***

"You look nice," I said as he came downstairs. I brushed away a stray tear before he saw it. "Are you ready for all this? This is the beginning for us, today."

Jason reached out and took my hand. "Today is the beginning. I like the sound of that. It's time. I haven't always been the greatest supporter in all this fertility stuff, as you know, but I promise today, I am with you. Okay? It's going to be fine. I am even kind of excited. Whatever the doctor says, we will be okay. I love you and we'll get through this."

It felt so nice to hear him say those words, "I'm with you."

The drive to Dr. Peterson's office was uneventful—no traffic, all green lights. I was hoping it was a sign of things to come. All good news. The office was empty when we arrived. After signing in, we were immediately brought back to a small examining room. A little larger than the room I had been in on my last visit. This room had an examining table, a desk and three chairs. The wallpaper looked fresh and the lighting was a little softer. Was this the room where they brought people to break bad news?

A short knock. "Hello again, young lady," came Dr. Peterson's voice. "And you must be Mr. Mathews. It's nice to meet you." Dr. Peterson extended his hand to Jason, who shook it quickly, then returned his own hand to his lap.

"Well, now. The results…" He was sifting through a small manila folder on the top of his desk, his reading glasses perched at the bridge of his nose. "Uh-huh. Yep. Fine." I stared eagerly as he perused the paperwork, obviously seeing the results for the first time.

"So?" I said impatiently. "What's the news?" My right leg bounced on the floor nervously. Jason put his hand over my kneecap to quiet the movement that was shaking both my chair and his.

Setting his glasses down on the desk, Dr. Peterson looked over at us. "Well, from the results I have in front of me, it looks like all is well."

That's it?

"All is well? So I'm okay?" I looked at Jason, who appeared to be losing the color in his face. He never did well in hospitals, and the faint smell of pine cleaner or bleach was filtering through the vents into the room. "Now what?"

"Well, now we send you to a specialist, and he will run a gamut of tests on you, Mr. Mathews." He looked down again at his notes. "May I call you Jason?"

"Sure. So, where do I go for the…the…test thing?" he asked apprehensively. I squeezed his hand. This was not any easier for him than it had been for me. I wanted both of us to be fine. I was still reeling with the possibility that it could be a problem with him. I was okay. I was okay.

Dr. Peterson rifled through the file drawer and pulled out a plastic bag. "Here's a sterile container and some paperwork with instructions. The rest is up to you," Dr. Peterson grinned. Man joke. Penis thing. Don't come right out and say it, Doctor, or he might just faint. Don't tell him that he is going to have to jerk off in a plastic jar—he knows. It's why he's been avoiding the whole thing. He's so afraid his little men are not marching right. Okay, I should have been feeling sorry for him, for both of us, but I was just so happy that I was fine.

"All the instructions are right there…no…the yellow sheet…yes," said Dr. Peterson. "It's important to abstain from ejaculation at least two to three days prior to collecting the sample." He said it. Jason shifted in his seat—crossing leg over leg and back again. "They like you to actually go into the basement clinic and provide the sample, but I do give you the container with the option of doing it at home."

Jason nodded. "Okay." At least I knew he was actually listening. Dr. Peterson said he would call to let us know when the appointment was with the urologist who would give Jason more details.

"If you do collect the semen sample at home, be sure to have it into the laboratory within an hour. The urologist's office will give you instructions on where to go. That is most important," Dr. Peterson rambled. Jason never blinked. "Keep the sample in your shirt pocket, close to your skin, to keep it warm. Then we do it all again in a few weeks, and you get the results—we'll know by the middle of next month. Any questions?"

Jason wiped his brow where the beads of sweat were clustering and stood to leave. "Nope. Got it. Thanks." He was at the door, container in hand, in a flash. I shook the doctor's clammy hand and followed.

***

On the day that Jason was due to bring in the sample, he was awake early and ready to go. I volunteered to tag along, for moral support, but he was ready and willing to go solo. It was encouraging to see the enthusiasm, even though I could tell he was a bit nervous about the whole experience.

"I will handle this one on my own," Jason said with a hint of a smile. "Just please don't run over and share the news with Josie just yet. Can you let me get to the lab before you dart across the street—if not for me, then for my boys?" He was actually lightening up about it now, after the initial shock had worn off. It only took him three days, but he was up for it. He was actually sounding anxious to find out. Or maybe he was just desperate for the sexual release? Who knew with men. They did think about sex every nine seconds—I remember reading that somewhere or seeing it on *Oprah.*

"I promise. I'll wait 'til I know you are safely around the corner before I rush over." I laughed. It was nice to smile again with him. The drastic transformation from the ostrich-in-the-sand attitude to this new proactive equal partner was astonishing.

I watched the clock—two minutes...three...four—that should give him plenty of time to get down the block. Grabbing my purse, I headed for the door.

Ten

"In prosperity, our friends know us;
in adversity, we know our friends."
—John Churton Collins

"Good morning!" Josie's voice boomed over the phone. "Up for some company?"

It was day two, D-Day, when the results of Jason's test would be in. The doctor had promised to call as soon as he had them. As the minutes ticked by at a snail's pace, I felt increasingly nauseated, lightheaded, yet very excited.

"Sure," I told her. "Come on over, I don't have anything to do today. Just a little housecleaning, junk like that," I tried to sound casual, as though I didn't have a worry in the world. Sometimes I wondered if she was sick of my constant ups and downs. I mean, really, when I thought about it, I wondered what attracted her to our friendship. Was it my obsessive qualities, or perhaps my innate sense of dread and doom?

"I'll throw on some clothes and be right over," she said.

My mind had been racing all morning with thoughts of babies, past and future. I turned on the TV and came upon yet another diaper commercial. Driving to the grocer yesterday, I passed three cars with the "Baby on Board" signs dangling from the back window. I couldn't stop thinking about my baby, my child. What did she look like now? Would she hate me for giving her up? Did she ever think of meeting me? When Jay and I first married I thought of searching for her; the secret weighed so heavily on me that I didn't know if I could lift it. I tucked that secret safely back in its little hiding place, but it changed nothing. I saw flashes of her face every day; images of her face scrolled across the inside of my eyelids, especially when I was tired and needed to sleep. Even now, after all these years, her face seemed so clear and brand-new to me. I blinked several times, trying to erase visions of her face.

I started a fresh pot of coffee and pulled a month-old package of frozen muffins out of the freezer. I hadn't been sleeping well, going over all the scenarios in my mind. I'm a chronic worrier, so those last few nights before the tests were spent playing the "what if" game with Jason. That is, until he insisted that I keep quiet so he could get some sleep. I kept myself company with Jay Leno, Conan Something-or-other, and a mindless program featuring half-naked women being interviewed by a horny talk show host. Eventually, exhaustion prevailed, but the last thing I remember was a commercial for a diet pill that promised to "flush away all the fat."

Josie arrived wearing a long black wig, a black and silver gown and spiked silver heels. She let herself in, as usual, without knocking. I don't remember when we shed this formality, it just happened. Family never knocked on doors and, other than Jason, Josie was the only family I had. "I'm afraid to ask," I said, shaking my head and smiling at her disguise. "I'm hoping this is your Halloween costume." The black hair was startling, though she wore it well. With the subtlety of a chameleon, she could transform herself into whoever she wanted to be. My friend was a woman who reveled in change. Just last summer, for about six weeks, her hair was strawberry blonde, and then, when the shock wore off, she changed it back. Josie loved to shock people and often said that it wasn't any fun if you couldn't get a rise out of someone. Always up for a challenge, always wanting to push the limits, Josie was not what you'd call *average.*

As funny and lighthearted as she was, she was also very pretty. Her delicate features—high cheekbones, brilliant blue eyes and tiny nose—were complemented by her full figure and creamy skin, giving her an exotic look. When Josie entered a room, she filled the space with her personality, no matter what her size or shape or color of hair.

I, on the other hand, was happy to blend in, and my dirty-blonde hair and average features helped me do just that. I enjoyed being average; I couldn't even imagine being "shocking."

So Josie was in my kitchen, twirling around, the black cape floating behind her. She tried out a witch-like cackle and Christopher clapped and chortled.

"Ya like it?" she asked. "It's Christopher's first real Halloween, isn't that amazing? I can't wait to see him trick-or-treating. Wait 'til you see the tiger costume I made for him. Cute! And believe it or not, I really did make it myself." She glided over to the coffee maker and fixed herself a cup. "Care to join us in some tricks and treats? I have this awesome cat costume that would be FABULOUS on you. Hell, with your skinny ass and long legs, you could land yourself some really great treats!"

I bent down and scooped Christopher up into my arms. "Boy, you are getting too heavy." I nuzzled him and whispered in his ear, "Did you know that your mommy was Looney Toons?"

More than eighteen months old now, Chris was a hefty guy. He took after his dad, whom I would describe as burly. So unlike Jason, who Josie once confided was a touch too *feminine* for her liking. "It's not that I don't love your husband," she told me, watching him arrange a fresh bouquet of spring flowers. I laughed loudly, knowing that anyone who didn't know him well might actually think he was gay. Even his voice had a softness to it that I found incredibly sexy, especially when he whispered in my ear. But what struck me as funny was that Josie blurted it out. Interesting, but this was one of the things I adored when I first met him: his soft side, his eye for detail and his love of everything beautiful. Oh, he had plenty of masculine qualities, most of which he displayed freely in our bedroom. I guess it excited me that he was such a mystery to people, yet I really "knew" him. As for that feminine side: I loved it.

There were, however, times when I wondered why I married him. But don't all couples feel that way?

"So, you find out today about the swimmers, huh?" asked Josie, taking Christopher from me and handing him a cold muffin. She pointed to the living room and I knew that she wanted to put the baby there, where he could eat and watch *Sesame Street.* Jason hated people, especially children, eating in that room. But I nodded, because I was anxious to talk about the "swimmers."

The clock read ten-thirty; it felt hours later. Josie read my jitters and said, "You know how it is with lab work, Paige. Not even God knows when they'll call. Hopefully, it will be today."

That's when I remembered her doctor's appointment. "I never did ask how you made out the other day," I said. "Did you mention my name to Peterson? Did he say anything to you?" I bit into the muffin, a sharp pain shooting through my tooth. "Damn, it's still frozen. Is Christopher okay with his?"

Josie shrugged and then peeked around the corner. "He's sucking on it, so you'll probably have to get out the vacuum when he's done." She took the muffin from me and dropped it into the toaster. "Don't you just hate those damn pap tests?" At that, she yanked off the wig. Her mousy brown hair was full of static and sticking out in all directions. A small bead of sweat lingered on her forehead. "Peterson never mentioned you, but we didn't talk much. I hate it when they talk into your crotch, anyway. It feels weird, don't you think, bending forward and looking between your own legs, while his head is down there, and you're trying to figure out what the hell he's saying. Shit, with that kind of intimacy, the guy should at least invite me to dinner afterward!"

I laughed, retrieved the toasted muffin, and took a bite. Without any warning, Josie sat down on the chair. I noticed that she was suddenly quiet, the light in her face having faded perceptibly. Before I could speak, she dropped the bomb.

"He found some lumps; I have to get a mammogram done right away."

I must have paled, perhaps my mouth dropped open, because she said, "I see that look on your face and don't go getting all weird on me. It's just a precaution, okay? I have lumpy boobs; that's it. He even said I could wait, but I want to get it over with."

Josie and I were polar opposites when it came to dealing with stress.

I was the eternal pessimist, while she was the never-ending optimist. I asked her once how she managed to keep things in perspective, how she remained so optimistic about things. She told me that she really believed that everything happened for a reason. Like it or not, there's a reason for everything, she said. I didn't share her optimism. I didn't really believe in all that fate stuff. I think life hands you a lot of bad deals and we all handle them our own way. She sees the glass as half full; I tend to see it as half empty most of the time.

This was definitely one of those situations where I forced myself not to show my panic. "So, when?" I asked. "When do you have the mammogram? And after that, what?"

"Tomorrow," she said. "So can you watch Christopher? I know you're busy, but I don't think the sitter is free and I'd much rather he stayed here." She paused for a minute, moved the salt shaker around. When she looked up, her eyes were almost round with fear. "It's no big deal, Paige, so stop looking at me like that! He said it's probably a blocked milk duct, from when I was breastfeeding, which makes perfect sense. This kid sucked so hard I sometimes thought he'd swallow me whole!"

I nodded. That was probably it, because she was way too young for—I couldn't even think the word, much less say it.

"He told me that lots of women get these and he just wants to be sure. You know how doctors are, always covering their ass in case it really is something."

I nodded at her. "Of course I'll watch him, just tell me what time." I had two appointments booked for that day, but Christopher often hung out with me in the basement while I worked. It was fun, and he loved putting on the capes and playing with the rollers. Josie had bought him a doll with a huge head of hair, and it came with mini-rollers, a brush, and a comb. While I worked, he worked, curling the wiry hair around the rollers, taking them out, putting them back in again. "Pretty?" he would say, which my clients loved, especially the elderly ones. I think being around small children made them feel young.

"It's the first appointment in the morning," she said. "But I might be there a while."

"Sure, just bring whatever he needs and we'll play hairdresser." A smile tugged at Josie's lips. Tom hated the hairdressing doll and was sure that playing with it would turn his son into a sissy.

***

I spent the rest of the morning cleaning the house, consciously distracting myself from everything else. I tried not to think about Jason's test results or Josie's startling news. The phone had remained silent the entire morning. I dusted and swept, rummaged through clothes and scrubbed down bathroom tiles—the cordless phone tucked into the pocket of my jeans. Not wanting to miss the call, I opted to skip the much-needed vacuuming. Just when I was ready to put the phone back on its cradle, it chimed loudly. Startled, I dropped the phone onto the kitchen floor where it landed with a loud bang. My heart danced in my chest as I reached down to retrieve the phone.

"Hello?" my voice crackled.

"Mrs. Mathews?" The voice on the other end was curt.

"Is Mr. Mathews at home? This is Dr. Crumb's office calling."

I cleared my throat, trying not to sound as frantic as I felt. "Uh...actually, he's at work, but I can give you his cell number." I don't know why we didn't give them that in the first place. There was a brief silence, a rustling, and then the monotone woman was back.

"That would be fine." I gave her the number, hung up and sat and waited. It wasn't long before the phone in my hand rang again.

"Hello?"

"It's me, babe," Jason said, no hint of emotion in his voice. Was that good? Was that bad? I didn't have time to even think about what it meant before he blurted it out. It was him. The results came back indicating a low sperm count. It was him.

"Are you there, Paige?"

"Yeah, I'm just...I can't believe it's...are you okay?" I thought of Jason talking to the nurse on the phone, being told that his sperm wasn't up to the job of getting us pregnant. Being a sensitive man, he would be devastated that he was the one. It would have been easier if it were me who had the problem. That, he could reason with, but this...

"I'd rather not talk about it...here. I'll see you at home later. Okay? I just wanted you to know." He sounded fine. Maybe I was just overreacting, again. After all, he had been trying so hard to be more open about the whole conception thing. I would make him his favorite dinner and then we could talk about what to do next. It would be fine.

"I'm heading over to Joe's after work. I'm sorry. I promised him I would help him move that dresser from his bedroom into Paul's. You remember the one? It weighs about a million pounds. I'll be back around eight...I'll see you then." The phone in my hand suddenly went dead. The only sound was a fuzzy tunnel-like echo.

Taking a deep breath, I quickly dialed Josie's number. It rang five times before the answering machine picked up. "You've reached the Fergusons! We're sorry we missed your call! It means so much that you try to keep in touch! Don't you fret, and don't you worry, we'll get back to you in a hurry! Toodles!"

Click! I was not in the mood for her sing-songy phone message. She changed it every month. I was surprised she hadn't recorded her Halloween message yet. It was usually a hit with all her friends who had children. Spooky, yet funny at the same time.

It was just two in the afternoon when I climbed back in bed. As I closed my eyes, I felt my body start to give itself over to the exhaustion. Vibrant colors danced behind my eyelids and at the end of a cascading rainbow, I saw his face. The grin was the same; both corners of his mouth turned up just the slightest bit. Shadow-like fingers stretched toward me...my body jerked. I inhaled deeply, squeezed my eyelids tighter and willed the vision out of my mind. You can't win. I won't let you win. A stray tear spilled from my eye. Shit.

Recalling the time Josie and I had found the rocking chair that now sits in Christopher's room put my mind at ease, and I felt the twisted muscles relax. *Think happy thoughts.* It was hilarious. The two of us in the wee hours of the morning rummaged through someone's garbage for hidden treasures. I had wanted to stay in the car, out of sight, but Josie was having trouble getting the barbells off the rocker. "Get your ass out here," she said, too loudly. I stuck my head out the window, putting my index finger to my lips in an attempt to shush her. "Get over here and help. Oh, for God's sake, no one will see you…" I quietly shut the van door behind me and helped Josie yank the rocker out from beneath the trash. Getting it into the van was another story. Between the two of us, we managed, but not until I got poked in the ribs by the dusty contraption. It was a scene straight out of *I Love Lucy*.

Man, she was too much. The rocking chair, stained a honey beige and refinished with a soft velvety seat, was the most comfortable seat in her house.

Eleven

"People take different roads seeking fulfillment and happiness. Just because they're not on your road doesn't mean they've gotten lost."

—H. Jackson Brown, Jr.

"I'll be back as soon as I can, pumpkin," Josie cooed at Christopher as she stepped out in the pouring rain. A cloud of exhaust fumes was escaping behind her car, the air getting colder by the minute. She looked up at me. "You're the best. I promise…no more chick appointments for a year, okay? I can't wait to see how my boob looks after they flatten it. I hope it pops back up! And I'm starving; I hope this guy has lollipops or something. Any idea what the 'booby prize' is for this kind of appointment?"

"I'm going to take him over to Jenny's Cafe for a chocolate milk and a cookie after I'm done with my last lady. Is that okay?" I set Christopher down on the floor; his little blue sneakers were digging into my thigh. A smile tugged at my lips; Josie knew how much I loved playing mommy at the shops with Christopher. My maternal juices flowed like honey when all the other ladies fell all over him. Some of them knew Josie, but the others assumed the blonde-haired boy was mine. He did actually look more like me than her. His chubby round face was always pink and warm. Josie's face was much more chiseled, even for her size. I was the short one—or petite, as Josie liked to call me.

"You're a shrimp, but I love you anyway. But, you do have legs, girl! For a short chick, you got great legs! What I would do for a pair of great legs," she said one day when we were trying to find a pair of dress pants that were short enough in the legs and that had a crotch that met mine instead of sagging to my knees. She saw my frustration and giggled. "You're just petite. It's a good thing. Look at me? Flat ass, thin waist, fat thighs, and big boobs…don't get me started with my disproportionate body. I would give my right arm for petite."

It had made me feel better. Shrimpy didn't appeal to me at all, especially after trying on twelve pairs of pants.

Turning to the van, "Let me grab his car seat," she said. Dodging cold raindrops, she unbuckled the seat and set and carted it over to my front porch.

"Thanks. If we're not here, we'll be there, at Jenny's. Good luck." I put my arms around her, gave her a short squeeze. "Go on now, lumpy…you'll be late."

Without another word, she was gone. I watched her drive away, knowing she was probably a little more scared than she let on. As close as we were, I always felt there was a whole other layer, like the old wallpaper that was in her hallway that I had not yet peeled away. I wonder if she felt the same thing about me?

***

Christopher's white cotton T-shirt now had the makings of a half a cup of chocolate milk, and even more chocolate slobber, all down the front. His face was chocolate encrusted and his tiny fingernails held bits of vanilla cream from a cookie. Not exactly the healthiest lunch for a little tyke, but it worked today. The drawing in front of him looked like a cross between a mound of colored worms and those big round flat lollipops that you can buy at the county fair. I had asked the waitress to bring lots of colors and Christopher had tried out every one in his masterpiece. It was spectacular!

"It's beautiful," I said, running my hand over his silky hair. He swatted at my hand. I was obviously distracting his concentration.

"Good job." I resisted the urge to put my nose on the back of his neck and inhale his baby scent. It was the place where angels kissed babies, I read somewhere once—the back of their necks. Ever since that day, I always smelled the back of a baby's neck when I was able to hold one in my arms. It was a heavenly scent. The best way that I could describe it is that it sort of smelled like sunshine.

In the reflection off the chrome napkin holder on the table, I caught sight of Josie as she came through the front door. She saw us right away, and Christopher saw her. My mommy-moments were long forgotten now that the real mommy had returned.

"Coffee, please," she motioned to the waitress behind the counter before sitting in the chair across from me. "Before you even ask...it was a piece of cake."

"Did it hurt?"

"No, it didn't really hurt. It was just weird. They put your boob between these two pieces of plastic and then squeeze them together. It just pinches for a minute. It hurt a little under my arm after it was done, but I'm fine now." Josie accepted the hot cup of coffee from the waitress and settled back in the chair. "God, I need this. I am outta fuel."

"Well, that's done. I bet you're relieved. When will you know the results?" Between the two of us, we were keeping the laboratories in Des Moines in business.

"Oh, you know, they give you their standard line—'Your doctor will call you in about ten days with the results,'" Josie said. "I mean I tried to turn to watch the technician's expression but she kept shoving me around. I couldn't even cheat. So, what's new with you?"

I hadn't had time to tell her about the latest round of test results we had gotten back about Jason. "Well...we got the results back on Jay's test...and it's not good."

Josie stretched her hand across the table and put it over mine. "Oh, Paige...I'm sorry. So, what now?"

I shrugged. "I'm not sure. I think they want him to do another test—to get another count—and then we go see the specialist. The nurse is setting up an appointment in the city with a reproductive endocrinologist. The test says that Jay's sperm count is extremely low with forty percent mobility—whatever that means. I guess they aren't moving fast enough to get where they need to go."

"How's Jason taking it?" Josie knew him well enough. Last night he came home late, relayed to me what the nurse said, and then said he was tired. I knew it was a huge blow to his ego.

"I don't know. I think he figures that baby-making is women stuff, like he doesn't really have a part in it. I know he's irritated that he has to do another test sample, and God knows what they will tell us after that," I said, trying to keep my voice low. We were the only three left in the place, everyone else having rushed home to make her hubby's dinner. "This is only just beginning and I am already sensing his resentment. I know it will be worth it, but it's not going to be easy."

I looked down at Christopher, who had squirmed his way out of the chair and was happily coloring on the leg of the table. "It's worth it. Trust me…it's definitely worth it. And I know it's going to happen for the two of you and then you both will be so glad you did all this, even the testing junk," Josie said, peeking under at her son. "When I look at him, my heart fills up so much that sometimes I think it just might explode. It's a love that can't be described until you feel it."

I know, Josie. I know. I know that feeling. It's a physical ache in my soul every day—remembering that feeling. I know, Josie, and I know how it feels to look into the eyes of the most beautiful baby in the world. I know how it feels to want something so badly that your body cries out in agony. I know how it is to love beyond words. "I'm sure there's nothing like it. I know it will happen if it's right. You know, as much as I hate some of the things in my life right now…I know there's a reason for everything. God, I think your optimism is rubbing off on me!"

"You said it!"

"We all have this path to walk, I guess, and I don't think it's supposed to be easy, do you?" I asked her.

"Well, I don't know about that, but I do think we can take our bumps and bandage them up, and try again," she said. "If you don't get up, if you stay down, that's when it gets tough. That's when you get trampled on, bruised and battered. Ya just gotta get up and get moving again."

"When I think back to the rape…and after, I thought I would die. I didn't, obviously, but it changed me in a way that I can't describe. It added this extension to me that I have to keep addressing. Would I change it? Yeah, I probably would change some of the past—but it's the bad stuff that makes the good stuff so damn good." As I spoke those words, I was trying to convince myself of their validity more than anything.

"My…you are philosophical today." A smile crept over her face. "What got into your cereal this morning? You been watching Dr. Phil again?"

"Shut up! It must be the coffee. Was it your special brew? A little bit of Josie added in?" I said. "Well, I better get home."

"Here," she handed me a pink envelope. "I'm having this party. My sister is coming and she insisted I have this ridiculous party. I guess she went to one last year and absolutely flipped over the products, so…of course I got suckered into it. Thankfully the wallpapering is done, and my new dining room furniture is coming next week, so I will have somewhere to put food."

Curious, I ripped open the cotton-candy pink envelope to find a similar pink-colored invitation:

For Women Only
Hostess: Starla Lane
Date: November 5th
Time: 6 p.m.
Where: 1080 Cedarwood Avenue
Maple Grove

Bring along your sense of adventure, imagination and creativity for a fun-filled evening just for the ladies! For Women Only is the largest home party based business for lingerie and more. Everyone from the very wild to the mildest of mild will enjoy the goodies I have to share. Please bring an appetizer to share. Don't be late—the fun begins at 6.

"I'm afraid to ask," I said, tucking the invitation into my bag. "What IS it? Should I be scared?"

Josie laughed. "Nah…not scared. It'll be a hoot. A nice break for both of us. We could use a laugh, right?" Josie scooped Christopher up; the chocolate on his shirt had bled down and was now a huge stain. "You know my sister, if there's anything in this world she is missing, she will just die. So I guess they have some premier products out, and she thought we would enjoy it."

"We? She included me? I just assumed you wanted me to come along to keep the two of you from killing each other."

Josie and her sister were as far apart as two sisters could be. I used to envy her, having a sister—until I met Judith. She was a cross between Atilla the Hun and Hannibal Lechter. "No, really. She said that you really needed to come." Josie grinned. "I think she feels it may help you—you know, sexually speaking."

Now I was laughing. "Yeah, I could see her saying that. Judith, not Judy…right?" I'd met the girl only twice before and both times I called her Judy and she practically tore my eyes out for it. "Well, she does know *everything* after all—surely she can help us create a baby."

"Trust me, she will have all the answers for you. She'll tell you that you are doing it wrong, or that you need to stand on your head after—God knows what she will come up with," said Josie. "I'm glad you don't let her bug you, though. And, yes…I do need you to be there so I don't wring her neck when she calls me Josephine!"

Twelve

"Laughter gives us distance. It allows us to step back from an event, deal with it and then move on."

—Bob Newhart

A cold wind whistled through the trees. In the distance, a lawnmower sputtered and coughed before finally coming to life. Fall was a beautiful time of year—my favorite time of year. Not too hot. Not too cold. Soon enough, the roads would be covered in a blanket of snow. Today was Josie's biopsy. The word biopsy even sounded cancerous to me. Josie was assured that she was low risk, prior to the mammogram, so I was hoping that this was just a further precaution.

"Are you ready to go?" I asked Josie over the phone. Tom had offered to take her, but Josie wanted me to go, saying it would be a good opportunity for father and son to have some time to play. I was glad she wanted me to come; I wanted to be there.

"Ready as I'm ever going to be." Her voice sounded cool and calm, like she did this every day.

"Be right there."

***

After Josie had donned the gently used, bluish-green surgical gown with the opening in the front, the nurse said I could go and sit with her. The room smelled vaguely of pine cleaner with a hint of something that resembled the scent of my lilac bush in the spring. The lights were too bright, the curtains that hung over the ceiling-high windows were stained in several places, and I was praying that the smudges on the wall were not blood. My first instinct was to whisk my friend away from the horrid place.

"Here, take this…no jewelry allowed," said Josie, handing over the mother-and-child necklace that her husband had given her for her first official Mother's Day. "You like the new look?" Josie opened and shut the gown, the bare skin of her breasts exposed to me in brief flashes of flesh. Not at all shy, Josie didn't think twice about calling me into the room if she was changing. We went shopping once, and she wanted to share a room, but I just couldn't do it. Modesty was my middle name.

"It's definitely your color. What *is* that color anyway?" Josie laughed. Whatever color it was, it made her look sick. You would think they could come up with a brighter, healthier color for those gowns. Who wants to wear something that sucks the color out of your face when you are about to go under the knife?

The door opened and the surgeon entered, wearing a similar shade of puce. After extending his well-manicured hand to me as an introduction, he explained to Josie that they were about to set up her intravenous, since she had requested to be sedated for the procedure. "I don't want to hear, smell, or even vaguely imagine what they are doing to my boob. Call me a wimp, but I even hate getting my teeth cleaned!" she had said to me.

After they had her all hooked up, they asked me to leave. "Well, I'll see you when you wake up," I told Josie, who was already beginning to look dozy. I leaned down and gave her a quick squeeze and a peck on the cheek. "Don't be too long, I got things to do, okay?" One corner of Josie's mouth curled upward in an attempt to smile.

It was well over two hours before I heard Josie's name being called. "Anyone here for Josie Ferguson? Is Josie Ferguson's ride here?"

Putting down the tattered copy of *Vogue* magazine, I announced my presence to the nurse in the doorway. She led me back to the same room where I had left Josie. There I found her awake and somewhat alert. I had expected to find her much groggier than she was. "How are you doing?" I asked her as I pulled the chair closer to the makeshift bed she was on.

"Fine…a little sleepy," she said, sitting up a little higher. "Ah, and sore." She placed her hand over her right breast and rubbed it a little. "They told me it would hurt a little for a day or so, and that's it." Just then the doctor waltzed into the room, every hair on his gray head in place, his chiseled good looks right out of a magazine. He flashed his perfect smile in my direction. Not sure if he was flirting or sharing his new porcelain veneers with me. The air was definitely reeking of arrogance, but I guess he was good at what he did.

"Hello again, is it Ms. Matthews?" asked Doctor Wonderful. "She did great. It was a fairly quick procedure, as I explained to Josephine. We removed the lumps, and now we wait. I've sent the tissue sample to our pathology department. We should know in a few days."

I don't know why I expected the doctor to just come in and immediately tell us that all was well. It felt a little anticlimactic. I guess I just figured that we would go over the test results, the x-ray kind that look so impressive on the lighted board, and he would laugh about Josie's lumpy boobs.

Doctor Wonderful patted Josie on the shoulder. "Anything else I can tell you?" The fluorescent lighting seemed to give his face a bluish-gray tint. I glared at him and he turned away, oblivious to my distaste at his nonchalant attitude. I know the guy did this every day, but we didn't.

Josie just shook her head. The nurse told her to get dressed. "We'll call you," she added as she left the tiny room. Another perfectly impersonal encounter from the medical community

I always thought I would be good at comforting someone if they needed me. I thought I had that inner maternal instinct or whatever it was that women had that prompted them to want to care for someone in need. As I stood there in that office, looking at my friend, my strong friend, I was seized by a sickening fear. I was totally unprepared when she started to cry—softly at first, so I didn't even realize she was crying. Then, harder—uncontrollable sobbing that spilled out in pitiful waves.

I reached over and grabbed her hand—I didn't want to hug her too hard. When her hand touched mine, it was as though her pain was transferred to me.

"Let it out, Jo. It's okay to be scared. You're allowed to be afraid," was all I could manage to say to her before we were both sobbing. Crying worked the same way that laughing did—ironically—it was one of those contagious emotions. Try as you might, just seeing someone you love in pain can start the chain reaction of tears that has both of you in the throes of an all-out tidal wave of tears.

***

"Favorite bumper sticker?" Josie asked. We were carving out the pumpkin for her front step and playing our "what's your favorite..." game. We had just discovered that Josie's favorite kind of lingerie was pajama pants—the loose, baggy kind from *Victoria's Secret*—and a T-shirt, no bra. Sexy.

"Yeah, the best line you have ever read on a bumper sticker?" I said.

"Like I would remember...hmm...Okay, let me think. I don't know if it's my favorite 'cause I can't say I have been taking notes, but I did remember one I saw last week that was funny." She tossed the empty margarita mix bottle into the trash. We had devoured almost a pitcher in a mere hour and a half. "It was on a Mercedes and it read, 'WAS HIS.'"

"That's a good one. My all-time favorite, and I do keep track...is 'Love may be blind, but marriage is a real eye-opener!' I had to chuckle again when I said it. I remember the exact moment when I pulled up behind the car that boasted this sticker on its rear end. I had just finished talking with Jason on my cell phone about the sample he was supposed to drop off at the lab. He claimed he was just too busy this month—it would have to wait. We've waited this long, he had said, what's another week or two? He had lost a couple of clients, he said, and he couldn't blow this new deal, something like that. I think I tuned him out sometime after he complained about not having time. I had just about slammed into the red Honda that bore the timely bumper sticker. The words seemed to jump off the bumper, like a sign from God. Was He trying to tell me something? Was He reminding me that my husband was a useless tit? Some might say I was overanalyzing, but I believe that there are signs all around us that we miss on a daily basis that guide us in certain directions in our life. I seem to keep missing the sign that says "Caution ahead."

"I love it!" Josie roared. "It's an eye-opener, all right? Ya know how Tom handled the biopsy thing?" Her voice was starting to sound like she had a mouth full of marshmallows. The margaritas were taking effect. I smiled as I watched her head bobbing a little. "Oh, he was a peach…the man that he is…he was a peach." She tipped her cup and sucked the salt off the rim of the glass.

I was losing her fast. I had had just one glass, not wanting to intoxicate my eagerly awaiting eggs, in case they were needed at any point in the next few days. Nothing worse than sluggishly hung-over eggs. "What did he say?" I was curious. I had steered away from the biopsy conversation for the entire evening, unsure of how much she wanted to talk about the whole thing. It was already four days after the surgery, and still no word. "No news is good news," is what people would say—God, I hate it when they say that. When people say that, you know it's because they are not sure what else to say. What do you say to someone? "Gosh, I hope you don't have cancer?" or "I wonder why it's taking them so long? What do you think is wrong?" People are so damn terrified of not knowing what to say—just like me.

"You know he's a gooooood guy," she said, emphasizing her words. "Most of the time, he says the right thing—but this time? I come home and he's here with Christopher and he doesn't even ask me how it went! Can you fucking believe it?" Tom was at his monthly poker night and Christopher was in bed. We had planned to carve out all the pumpkins, but had only managed to cut out one eye and part of the mouth of the first one.

"No? He didn't even ask you? I can't believe it!" I brought the empty glasses to the sink, and noted that it was already well past eleven. "So, what *did* he say?"

"He said that he and Christopher had fun playing Nintendo—like my baby is playing Nintendo? The big lug played video games the whole time I was under the knife, I'll bet." She brushed the hair out of her eyes and almost toppled over onto the carpet. "Cute, huh?"

"Wasn't he the least bit curious? Maybe he was afraid to ask—you think?" Josie looked at me as though it never dawned on her that her husband would be a little frightened about the procedure. "You know," I continued. "Tom is a good man. He probably is afraid to ask you. I bet he thinks that if you don't tell him, then everything must be fine. I bet he just thinks it's woman stuff."

Josie flattened out on the carpet and stared up at the ceiling. "You think so? I mean he did take care of me this past week after I told him it hurt to lift heavy things." Josie's gaze drifted sideways toward the darkness outside the living room window. Nothingness. There was nothing to see. "Maybe you're right. He did say not to worry…until we know."

"See, he is just trying not to freak you out because he knows it will all be fine."

"I guess so. You know, I'm not really freaked out anymore, anyway. It was just so weird in the office. It was so damn clinical; it almost felt like I could *catch* cancer just by being there. It was an eerie feeling." The C-word was out. I wished I could retrieve it. I had hoped that maybe if neither of us said it, it wouldn't become real. Josie didn't even flinch, though it was the first time that either of us had uttered the word. All of a sudden I felt clammy—my stomach did a somersault. Probably the margarita making its final descent.

Josie looked at me, a smile tugged at her lips. "Well, you know what they say, 'No news is good news.'"

Thirteen

"Courage is grace under pressure."
—Ernest Hemingway

The message light was flashing on the answering machine when I returned from the library. I had ventured out in the rainy weather to find some books on cooking, in hopes of creating a gourmet meal to set the mood for a night of seduction. Maybe it's true; maybe I can get to his heart through his stomach.

The light on the answering machine was blinking relentlessly. I stopped and stared at it: WARNING, WARNING, the orange glow flashing to a rhythm. I clicked the button. "Paige...Paige...you there ...of course you're not there...I'm looking out my window and I can see you're not there. Can you call me when you get in...doesn't matter how late, I'll be up."

Josie's voice sounded different. It was a tone that I was not used to hearing. I had heard it once before, but I couldn't put my finger on when. Was it when she was working on that new project and was freaked out when the craft store was out of red glitter, or was it the tone she used when Tom left his work clothes on the new cream-colored carpet? For a woman who avoided negativity like the plague, her voice was definitely not as upbeat as usual. Her voice was always full of emotion. I loved that about her. If someone asked me to describe Josie in one word, I would have to say Josie was *alive*. That was how I saw her—more alive than anyone I knew.

I picked up the phone to dial just as the front door closed with a bang. "Paige?" came Josie's voice from the front hallway. Setting the receiver back in its cradle, I walked over to meet her.

"Hi there. I was just about to call you." I tried to sound so casual. Maybe I was overanalyzing the message. My eyes swept quickly over her face, searching for something, anything that would indicate that I was not about to hear what I didn't want to hear. Her hair was tucked back with a red and white tartan headband and her clothes were a mess. She wore green tennis shoes, no socks, sweat pants and a wrinkled red T-shirt that looked like they had been left in the dryer too long. Josie was not a clothes hound, but she usually looked put-together. She actually made looking good seem effortless. Always the right shoes with the right handbag, even if it was a 2-for-1 Payless special.

"Hey, Where's Christopher?"

Josie kept walking, without answering me. She walked all the way through the living room, the dining room and rounded the corner to the kitchen. She opened the fridge and grabbed one of the wine coolers that was left over from a month ago when we had our ladies night out, when we stayed in. It always ended up being more fun when we hung out just chatting over a wine cooler or a pitcher of margaritas. Lately, though, we used the occasion to mourn another pregnant-free month. She was always there whenever I had those moments of despair—which seemed more frequent these days. Sometimes I didn't know how she put up with me.

She turned to me. "It's not good, Paige. It's cancer," she blurted out as she popped the top on the sweaty bottle. Just like that. I just nodded like an idiot, my mouth hanging wide open. The wind rattled against the kitchen window, the refrigerator hummed a familiar tune and a truck backfired down the road; the sounds of everyday life were suddenly loud and present, as though they'd been muffled all those years by my naive expectation that they would always be there. Josie had cancer.

I looked up from my dazed stupor to find her looking at me, waiting for me to say something, say anything. As I looked into her eyes, I saw a longing I had never seen before. "No. No, it can't be." I said, tears forming in my eyes. "I don't know..."

"Hey. No, don't do that. Paige, it's okay," she said, comforting me. She put her arm around my shoulders. "It's okay. It's not every day someone tells you they have the big 'C'. No crap. I can do this. I will do this. I'll beat it. So don't you get all crazy on me, you promise? That I can't do."

I sniffed, tears poured down my cheeks. "I'm sorry," I said. My voice sounded like it was coming from inside a tunnel. All the emotions of the past month were finally bubbling to the surface. A sharp pain shot across my forehead as I suppressed the urge to scream.

A sudden but distant memory of Suzie Long, my best friend in the fourth grade, flashed before my eyes. We were holding hands on our way to school. "We'll always be friends, right?" she was asking me. I was nodding, and chewing on a wad of pink passion bubble gum. "Promise me. Promise we'll be friends forever and ever." *Of course we will,* I had told her. Forever and always, nothing will keep us apart. But forever is a really long time.

Every part of me was chilled, as if the temperature in the room had plummeted the moment she announced her diagnosis. "Are you scared?" I asked, wiping my nose with the Kleenex she had got for me. She shrugged at the question. *What a stupid question.*

She took a drink of the cooler. "Can you take me to see the doctor tomorrow? He wants to give me the gory details in person, I guess," she said, sounding more and more like Josie. I just kept staring at her, searching for what might be different. "Whatever happens, whatever they have to do, I'll do it. You aren't getting rid of me yet, chick, so stop staring at me like I have one foot in the grave, would ya? Geez. Just don't."

I nodded. "Yeah, of course." Then I thought of Tom. God, he must be reeling. "What does Tom say about it?"

"I haven't told him yet. I couldn't reach him. I paged him and tried his cell phone but he must be in the building. I can't get him when he's inside the plant." She hesitated then, as though she wanted to say more, but didn't. "I'll wait 'til he gets home, after Christopher is in bed. We can't talk when he's up; the little rascal is so busy these days. He's playing at Suzanne's house right now."

"Yeah, probably best." I was numb. In her moment of crisis, I was numb. Nothing inspiring came to my mind. No comforting words of wisdom. Nothing.

"It's weird, you know, I mean, you just think you're always going to be fine. I take care of my child, I get plenty of exercise and I eat pretty well, so you just figure you're all right. Then, one day, you're feeding your kid a bowl of macaroni, the phone rings and your life is forever changed in the beat of a heart," she says in a quiet voice. "I know I'll be fine, this is just what I'm supposed to be fighting right now, I guess. Someone up there must think I need to kick some ass. Well, bring it on, I say." She smiled a Josie-smile and for a split second, all was well in the world again.

***

I landed a parking spot out front this time, which was a relief. Josie rushed ahead of me to check in, hoping to beat the old man who was hobbling on one leg towards the front door. You would think she was on her way to a show, fighting her way in to snag the last ticket.

"How long did they say?" I asked, settling next to her on the faded blue-floral sofa.

"There's just one person ahead of me, thank God."

"You could have held the door open for that poor man," I said quietly, nudging her as he walked past us, glaring.

"I guess I'm a little anxious," she said. "Shit, I could've died before the guy made it to the door."

I set my coffee down on the table, alongside all the health and fitness magazines. "So are you okay? Did you talk to Tom?" I was up half the night, evident by the dark circles under my eyes. I had let myself cry, quietly, trying desperately to release some of the pain I was feeling. I thought if I could just have one good cry, I could make it through the appointment without a hitch. It just had to be fine.

"He didn't take it so well. I think he was worse than you. You people are so encouraging. Please don't make funeral arrangements until they give me the prognosis, okay?" She smiled at me. "He was nagging me for more details and I just didn't have any to give him, which frustrated him. He got home really late and I was tired, so it was a short talk." Josie stood up. When I did the same, she said, "I'll be back in a sec. Too much coffee."

A woman in a yellow baseball hat took the chair across from us. She was stunning. Her eyes were a smoky shade of periwinkle and her flawless skin was peppered with the tiniest amount of makeup. She didn't need it. Her body was rail-thin, too thin. Hanging from her neck was a large glass locket. I was mesmerized by the way it reflected the light.

"It's pretty, isn't it?" said the woman, noting my interest.

I looked up and she was looking straight at me. I felt my face flush instantly. "I'm sorry...yes, it's very unique."

The woman leaned forward. "I keep a piece of my hair in it, to remember what it was like before all this." She pointed to her hat. I could see that she had no hair on her head and that her eyebrows were gone, too. I nodded, locking eyes with her. "I'm sorry."

"Sorry? No, don't be sorry," she stated, her back straightening. "I'm still here; nothing to be sorry about." The woman smiled and nodded at me.

Why did I suddenly feel so helpless? I mean, here was Josie, taking the whole thing in stride, acting like this was just a little detour on her way to the mall, and now this lady sitting here looking deathly ill, and she's smiling. How the hell could someone be smiling?

"Your first visit, huh?" the woman asked. "I was scared the first time, too. It just becomes so real when they tell you face-to-face. But you'll be fine, there are some amazing things they can do now."

I put my hand to my chest. "Me? No, no it's not me. I mean, I'm not—" My voice quivered. "It's my friend, it's Josie. She's the one."

"Ah." The woman nodded. "How's she doing?"

"She's fine; it's me that's a mess. She seems to be fine. But then, she's kind of like that. You know, one of those 'go with the flow' kind of women."

The woman adjusted her cap. "That will help, believe me. A positive attitude is the first step to recovery."

"Well, if anyone can beat it, she can." I smiled, thinking of the time when I came over to her house, distraught again about not getting pregnant. Josie had looked up at me, tears running down my face, and said, "You're going to get pregnant, you will. I just think your body is so damn picky, it's waiting for the perfect child. You wouldn't settle for anything less now, would you?" I had to smile; she knew me so well. If I didn't know better, I would've agreed with her. I've always wanted everything to be just right.

Josie had just sat back down when they called her name. She leaned over to me and grabbed my hand, giving it a squeeze. "Here we go. You with me?"

I nodded. *I'm with you, Josie. I'll always be with you.*

Fourteen

"We could never learn to be brave and patient, if there were only joy in the world."

—Helen Keller

Josie

I wore a black skirt and a red blouse when I met with the surgeon. A part of me wanted to look so stunning that the surgeon would just take one look at me and declare, "I'm sorry, this has been a huge mistake. You don't have cancer—look at you, you are amazing! The picture of health." Like a cheap skirt that I found hidden at the very back of my closet would make *all* the difference. Paige looked absolutely gray when she came to pick me up. If the girl got any stiffer, I swear she would break into a million pieces. But I loved her for being afraid for me. What more could you ever ask for in a best friend? I didn't even have to worry; she was doing enough for both of us.

"So..." said the doctor in the fancy lab coat. "I'm sorry we had to give you such bad news." He shifted in his chair, redistributing his weight from one ass cheek to the other. Hemorrhoids, I'll bet—been there.

"Yeah, me too, Doc. I mean, it was a shock, it kind of floored me, you know?"

"Well, Mrs. Ferguson, I received the complete report from the pathology department. The results of your biopsy were not what we had hoped."

"So they say…what now?" I looked over at Paige, who had her winter black purse clasped tightly in her fists. She must have just switched to her autumn colors. She always had to match the seasons with her shoes and purses. Spring was the off-white shoulder bag with the beige penny loafers, summer was a straw bag with the sling-back sandals (her favorite), autumn was the brown handbag and brown mules, and of course in winter she loved wearing her long black heeled boots along with her black alligator-print purse. God help us if she was seen with an autumn purse in the spring!

"Well, I don't know how to say this gently, Mrs. Ferguson…" the doctor began.

"Can you call me Josie, please?" The doctor was struggling, and it was making me nervous. Think of something worse…think of something worse.

"Josie…it doesn't look good…the cells are very abnormal and they are poorly undifferentiated." I continued to stare at him. "I'm recommending a mastectomy followed of course by a round of chemotherapy and radiation therapy."

"What is the prognosis…after the surgery and treatment? What is the survival rate on this kind of cancer, at my age?" I had searched the Internet, read every paper, report and study I could find, but it was mind-boggling. I read that women who were younger than thirty-five had an increased recurrence rate and a lower percentage rate for survival. That did not encourage me.

"There's no way to know for sure…yet. I would feel better if you weren't so young. There is, however, new evidence to support an increase in survival rate when pre-menopausal women undergo surgery during a specific phase of their menstrual cycle. We'll go ahead and schedule your surgery based on your cycle."

"Well, then, let's do it. What do I need to do first?"

Paige let out a sigh, as though she had been holding her breath the entire time. I had almost forgotten she was there.

"First, do you have any other questions?"

"No, not really. When all this sinks in, I am sure I will. So, whom do I schedule the surgery with?" I wasn't wasting any time. After all the horror stories I had read online the night before, I was anxious to get rid of this cancer as fast as possible. Boxing gloves on, I was ready to fight this demon to its death. The doctor set me up with his nurse, who went over my records, charted my menstrual cycle, and determined that ten days later would be the best time to operate. *Ten days before I lose my breast.* "Just before Thanksgiving, but in plenty of time to be feeling like company by then, okay?" she told me. You could tell she had a heart filled with compassion for people. You don't do that kind of job—see terminally ill people all day—and act like a hard-ass. It just wouldn't work. Her voice was like silk, no edges. She spoke *to* me, not at me. I almost felt like I was scheduling my next haircut, it was so easy.

"Thanks. I'll be here at 5 a.m. then?"

"Josie, is there anything else I can tell you about all this? Here is my number, call me if you think of anything. Anything at all, " she said, placing her hand on my forearm.

"No, but thank you. I'll be fine. If I have any questions, I'll call." Paige held the door open and I slipped out into the waiting room, which was now filled to capacity with patients. *That's what I'll be for a while, yet another new title for me to carry around. Daughter, then wife, mother, friend, and now cancer patient. Well, I won't be wearing that hat for long.*

"How're you doing?" Paige asked as we drove out of the hospital parking lot. "I don't know what to say. I mean, I haven't known what to say. Is that dumb or what?" I had seen Paige's hand shaking as she turned the ignition. Her delicate pink fingernails were chewed down to nothing.

"No, it's not dumb. I don't know what I would say if I were you, either." It was true. I wouldn't know what to say. In some ways, I was glad it was me and not her. Not that I wanted to be sick, or have my breast removed, but if it were Paige, I don't think I could handle it. The very thought of losing her would be too much to bear. "Can we just talk about something else for a minute? I'm kind of on overload."

Paige turned to me then, her pale skin looking even paler. "Aren't you scared?"

"Who me?...I'm terrified. Now...enough." I rolled down the window, stuck my head out and closed my eyes to the sting of the wind.

"Sure. Okay," she said, turning the car radio on low.

"What about that silly party you are having next week? You still gonna have it? When is your sister coming?"

I had almost forgotten that she was coming, with everything else going on. I was in no way prepared to share my news just yet. Especially with my sister.

"Shit! She's coming day after tomorrow...shit! I don't know if I can deal with her right now. I haven't told anyone anything yet. You know what, can we just keep it to ourselves when she's here? I would rather wait until after the surgery. You know how she is anyway...useless ..." I had to laugh when I thought about my sister. Telling her that I was going to go and have a breast removed would be quite the shock. I remember the time she had a mole removed from her ass, you would think she lost a leg the way she whined about it. I wasn't up to it.

"Your call. Mum's the word." There was silence for the rest of the ride home, which was fine. Paige and I had the kind of friendship that had an easy intimacy—it didn't need words to sustain it. We could sit for over an hour on blankets in the yard and never speak. Watching clouds pass overhead or listening for the definitive sounds of all the birds that visited the trees in my backyard, we didn't need conversation to know what the other was thinking. There was a kind of internal calm that hung over us when we were together.

***

"Well now, hello there...it was Paige, wasn't it?" said Judith, the minute Paige stepped across the threshold. Her hand extended, she practically assaulted the poor girl. My sister had been here a mere eighteen hours and my living room furniture had been rearranged, my hairstyle was deemed unruly and immature, and my child was too skinny.

Paige offered her hand slowly, cautiously.

"Hi, Judith. It's so nice to see you again.

"Yes, it's been far too long. My sister never invites me to her 'small town.'" Judith said. She had obviously forgotten that this was the "small town" that she had been born and raised in. Judith had escaped our hometown years ago when a traveling salesman swept her off to California. The salesman is long gone, having run off with an Avon lady just a year after they were married, but Judith says she found herself in L.A. The city with bright lights got even brighter when my sister arrived there, I was sure. Even though I found her to be overbearing and obnoxious, she did light up a room. People were drawn to her, maybe out of sheer curiosity as to how this creature survived in the real world.

"Judith, can you lay off the guests! Geez…go grab another margarita. I made the frozen banana-strawberry ones tonight, just for you, babe." I winked at Paige. "Maybe I can get her drunk. I'm prayin' she'll pass out before the hostess gets here."

"I heard that!" Judith yelled back from the kitchen. I rolled my eyes at Paige, who couldn't help but grin. "Where is everyone?" she asked. The living room was set up with extra chairs to accommodate the guests for the "sex party" that Judith had dragged me into.

"I don't know. It's a little early. There really isn't a whole bunch coming. I mean, who am I gonna invite in this neighborhood? I'm guessing that old lady Winters doesn't have much use for a 'super-sized pre-lubricated dildo'!" The neighborhood was old, the neighbors were old; everything was just so old. It was the one thing I noticed just days after coming home from the hospital with Christopher. The oak tree in front of my house was old; the poor thing looked like it was waiting for the end, patiently watching as young saplings grew beyond the boulevard. Sometimes things are just ready to go; like the oak tree.

Paige was recovering from her snitter-fit of laughter when the doorbell rang.

"Hello there! Move on over! Lady with a load of lovelies coming through!" a woman's voice boomed at the door. Her arms were filled with bags and boxes of all shapes and sizes. "Oh, I'm Starla by the way, and you must be the lovely Josephine. Your sister has told me so much about you." She has? What on earth would Judith say about me? My hair was the wrong color, my hips were too wide, and I should've married the football player who offered me a mint one day at a game?

"Hello there, Starla!" Judith ran forward and engulfed the woman with a hug. Starla's platinum-blonde locks bounced as Judith squeezed. "We're all set up in the parlor, darling. I've just set out a tray of finger sandwiches and scones for our guests."

Soon, the guests started arriving, even Mrs. Stewart, the lovely lady next door. I was shocked to see her squeeze in past Carrie Dormidy. Mrs. Stewart and her husband had lived in the house next door longer than anyone on the street. They probably planted the old oak tree that sits on their own front lawn adjacent to mine. When she noticed that I had a baby, she had been the first one to bring me a meal, even before Paige. When she spoke, her voice warmed you. She was one of those people who made you always feel like everything was going to be all right.

The party was in full swing within thirty minutes. Echoes of laughter filled every corner of my little bungalow. It was nice to see Paige having fun. I caught her trying to figure out the vibrator that was appropriately named "The Frogger." She had instantly blushed all the way down to her bust line.

"Okay, ladies, now that you've seen all our gadgets and gear, I'm gonna go in the other room. Your order will be completely private," Starla was saying. To my surprise the first lady to jump up and cross the room was Mrs. Stewart. Catalog in hand, she was set to go. I stifled a smile.

"So, what are you buying?" I nudged Paige. "I hope you brought your credit card. This was fun, huh?"

"Yeah, I guess. It was…interesting. I think I'll buy some of the massage oil," she said. Massage oil was about as wild as I could expect Paige to get. I couldn't imagine she would walk out the door with the edible undies or the peek-a-boo satin bra. Although I bet Jason would love it if she did!

"Yeah, that's nice stuff. I have some. It smells wonderful. Maybe I will buy one of the sexy nightgowns. Lord knows I am going to need help when my hair starts falling out," I whispered to her.

"Are you going to at least tell her about it, Jo?" I knew she was talking about Judith.

"We really haven't had a chance to talk about me. Can you imagine that? She's been so busy filling me in on every detail of her Alaskan cruise, her new apartment and the handsome guy who lives upstairs. He's Swedish, you know. I didn't have the heart to tell her that I heard Swedes have little dicks."

"Josie, she has to know. She's your sister."

"Well, I decided what I'm gonna do is write everyone a letter. Just a short note to explain everything," I told her. "That way, I won't have to rehash the gory details over and over again. I just can't handle the looks, Paige. I mean, you even do it, and I know you don't mean to. It's the death look. I just can't do it right now."

"Can't do what?" asked Judith.

"Oh, just Thanksgiving stuff…it's a pain," I said, clearing away some of the empty glasses to avoid my sister.

"I know," she started. "Why, just last week, my dear friend and her family suggested that I host it this year at my new place. I was astounded. I mean, the girl has two children with incessant sinus problems…and I do have a suede sofa…what she was thinking I will never know…" Good old Judith, you could always count on my sister to turn everything around to be about her.

When the party guests finally left, I collapsed on the bed. Tom and Christopher wouldn't be back 'til morning. Grabbing the notepad out of my bedside table, I began to write the most important piece of writing of my life. A letter to my son. First that, then the Josie-cancer saga for my friends. First, I needed to tell my son.

Fifteen

"Don't walk in front of me; I may not follow. Don't walk behind me; I may not lead. Walk beside me, and just be my friend."
—Albert Camus

I was just throwing in a new load of laundry when it hit me. Just a day before the surgery, I had tried to keep as busy as possible with household chores, yard work and other things that I knew I wouldn't be able to do when I came home. I was scared to death. Paige had called three times and I promised her I was fine. Tom decided it was best if he just stayed out of my way today and he said he couldn't miss another day of work since he would have to take time off next week. Why did I feel so guilty? He hadn't said much to me about my cancer, hadn't even uttered the word. As a husband, he'd always been great to me, good at being home on time, not out carousing with the guys on Friday nights like some of the men at work, but he wasn't much of a talker. I always thought I was bad at talking about my real feelings, opting for sarcasm most times in place of sheer gut-wrenching emotion, but he was even worse. He was silent. When I told him about the mastectomy, he shrugged. "What the hell? Your wife tells you she has cancer and is having a piece of her body removed and all you can do is shrug?" I yelled at him.

"Babe, I can't begin to understand what you must be feeling, but from my end, I dunno what to do," he said. "I don't know how we're going to get through all this, with Christopher and everything, but I know in my heart that you'll be fine. But, there's a lot to think about. Like, what are we going to do with Chris all day while I'm at work? Who is going to take care of the house and all this junk?" He had pointed around the room at the toys that were scattered from corner to corner. I stood there staring at him for a moment, not sure how to respond. The anxiety of the surgeon's words was now completely masked by my own husband's asinine comments of self-absorption.

I hadn't shed a tear, and I wasn't about to do it for his benefit, not now. Not for him. "Well, asshole…I guess you'll have to hire someone! How dare you throw that shit at me now! What if I die, huh? What if you are left alone to deal with all this shit? Maybe you better start thinking about what you might do long-term if I'm not here," I shouted. "Jesus, Tom…I expected more of you. But, I guess it's true, what they say…you really learn about people when things get tough." I walked out of the room, unable to continue; my heart was racing so fast I thought it was going to burst through my T-shirt.

The warm tears rolled down my face unexpectedly now, just as the washer started to rotate. I laid my head down on the vibrating machine and sobbed. Finally letting go of the weeks of tension and fear. I had to be strong for everyone, it seemed, for Tom, for Christopher, for Paige, but not this moment. Right now, I cried and cried until there was nothing left. I cried for my breast—it was the bigger of the two, though I don't know why that mattered to me. It was the one I liked the best. Paige used to joke with me about it, the fact that it was almost a half size larger than the other. When I wore certain clothes, like bathing suits, you could really tell. She and I called my breasts "The Lopsy Twins," because they were so lopsided. I cried because we would never think of my breasts and laugh again. I cried for the loss, to never feel my husband's hand caress that breast again. *It will all be so different. Will Tom be able to love me when I'm not a whole woman? Jesus, now I know why they offer that post-surgical therapy. I better call that nurse and get my name on that list!*

I was just wiping my face on a clean, warm towel when I heard a knock at the front door. Christopher was sleeping, so I had to answer the damn thing. If it was a solicitor, they knocked first, and then blared the doorbell until they were sure that no human being lay hiding in the wake of their presence behind the door.

"Hi," Paige said, weakly, as I opened the door a crack, surprised that she had knocked. "Care for company? My last client just left and I can't stop thinking about you over here all by yourself…today. I wasn't sure…"

I flung my arms around her. I felt the tears rising, having had time to regenerate in my body, the salty liquid now flowed generously down my cheeks again. My body shook violently, as though I were freezing. Paige kicked the door closed behind her and led me to the sofa, never letting go of me. We sat like that, for a few minutes, and I finally broke free.

"I'm sorry. Just seeing you did it to me," I said, half-laughing at the nonsense of the statement. "I mean, I was just upstairs having a pity party and I was thinking I should have invited you. And now you're here…thanks. I didn't know I had all this in me. I really thought I was going to make it without freaking out, but something just burst inside me. I have an incredible headache from crying half the day. I gotta get some Tylenol or something. Would you like something to drink? Are you hungry?"

"No, no…I just wanted to see how you were doing. It must be hard, today. Is Tom with Christopher? I noticed his truck was home."

"No, he just started carpooling with this guy one street over from ours. He's trying to find a way to save a little money. I don't know…I don't think I have heard half of what the man has told me the last two weeks. He blabbers on about everything that has nothing to do with my cancer. He just can't handle it, Paige. I'm afraid." I was so afraid. I had heard that some men choose a cancer diagnosis as a one-way ticket out the door. Men leave all the time, unable to face the reality, the trauma, the new title of caregiver, or perhaps they are just not capable of seeing themselves with a one-breasted partner. It was not such a far-fetched concern.

"He's probably dealing with it in his own way— you always tell me men are just so different from us. Give him time—he'll come around."

"I don't have time! I need him to get with it now!" I yelled. Not meaning to yell at Paige, I felt so angry all of a sudden. "Sorry, don't mean to scream at you. Jesus, I'm just so mixed up. I really expected him to just be so supportive. But, hey, he's a guy, right...what was I thinking? I'll just have to do this on my own."

"Come on...you will never be on your own. I'm here. I will be here to help you. Geez, I can't believe you would say that," said Paige.

I could see that Paige was wounded by my comment. It was an insensitive thing to say. I just can't seem to win these days. "You have your own stuff to deal with, you don't need my stuff. Tom is right, what am I going to do with Christopher? He is off work for three days, but it is going to be a while before I can pick him up or anything. Maybe he is just being practical and I am being an idiot."

"You have friends, Jo. They will help you. I have cleared my schedule for the next two weeks...never mind, it's already done. What did you think? Did you actually think I was gonna sit back and not help you?" Paige said. "Come on...I hope you know me better than that."

Christopher's tiny footsteps distracted us, thankfully, from going deeper into the conversation. Since he got his "big-boy bed," his naps were getting shorter. Most kids stayed in their cribs for at least two years, but not my son. As stubborn as his mother, he decided a few months ago that the crib was not going to cage him in any longer. Out of pure fear of the child dropping onto his skull while trying to escape his nighttime prison, I decided it was time for a toddler bed.

"Hey, baby...there's my sleepy boy!" I exclaimed at the sight of him. He had his "tiny teddy" cradled under his arm—the one that Paige gave him on his half-year birthday. She was always surprising the child with one thing or another; all his rottenness, I told her, spawned from her excessive generosity and her permissive babysitting tactics.

"How are you doin', buddy? You look sleepy."

Christopher bowed his head in the usual bashful way he did whenever anyone spoke to him. It always took him a bit of time to warm up to anyone who was visiting, no matter how well he knew them. He was also at that very clingy age. I could barely get a shower in without him by my side.

"Well...I better finish up with my laundry, Paige. It's already, what...three o'clock and I haven't even washed the lunch dishes yet. I can't go to the you-know-where with dirty dishes in the sink!" I winked at Paige, a sign that I was going to be fine. It was safe for her to go.

"You don't want me to help?"

"Trust me, when I'm done with you, you will never want to see me again! I'm fine. I kinda want to putz around and just hang out with Christopher." I hated to ask her to leave, but I really wanted to cuddle up on the couch and let my son lay his head on me and just chill out for a bit.

Paige took the cue, and escorted herself to the door. "See you first thing," I yelled after her. "Don't be late!"

***

On the way to the hospital, I talked to Paige about the reconstruction surgery that they described to me. I declined the idea of having the reconstruction done at the time of the mastectomy. Somehow I didn't feel capable of making the decision, not yet. The whole thing sounded grotesque to me.

"I don't want skin from my ass being molded to make a new boob. It just doesn't seem right to me," I said to Paige. She winced. "I don't know. Maybe I will think differently when it's done, but right now...I can't even think about it. If it's one boob I have, then so be it. I would rather just get used to that idea, then decide."

"I'm sure it's done with skin from all over, whatever works best. Not just your ass." I saw her try to suppress a smile.

"I'm sorry, but the thought of it just freaks me out. I want to take my time on this decision. I already feel like I'm being rushed. A month ago I was just me—Josie Ferguson, wife, mother, and woman—and now I am a cancer patient. That sucks, but it's my reality. As much as I don't want that title, it's mine. I hope in time, it will fit." The doctor had explained that my cancer was apparently at a serious stage. I guess I should have found it earlier. I did those breast exams, like they tell you to, but I don't think I did them right. I wish I had asked. "So, how are you doing? Have I asked you? How is the baby-making going?"

"I'm fine. We have to go in for a consultation about in vitro and all that," said Paige. "I think we go next Friday. Another new doctor in the city."

"How is Jason? How is he doing?"

"He's doing good. I think his bruised ego is healing well. You know…the low sperm count and all. His male psyche went into testosterone shock when he found that out, but he's doing much better."

Knowing Jason as I did, I could see how he would react to that kind of news. He was the kind of guy who was threatened by even the slightest joke about his maleness, even though he was the most effeminate man I had ever met. Even when I would comment about his love of cooking, he would become offended. He was always on the defensive, couldn't take a joke.

My heart lurched a little at the sight of the hospital. I felt my breath quicken and inhaled deeply. There were no more tears. I had come to terms with the facts of the surgery. I had even taken a picture of myself with the web camera. Tom thought it was weird, my wanting a photograph of myself before the surgery. I felt as though I was memorializing my breast. He said I was morbid. I don't think men can fully understand how much a woman's breast is a part of her. I had never given it a second thought, never even noticed them until the diagnosis. Now, I couldn't help but wonder how much of my sexual being was identified with my breasts. Tom said I was overanalyzing it, but when I asked him how he would feel if I cut off his dick, he didn't think that was so funny.

The lady who was called my "Breast Pal" met me at the admissions desk. She went over all the pre-surgical stuff with me. When she was done with the rundown of what to expect after surgery, she slipped me her phone number. "Call me…day or night."

Sixteen

"Hold a true friend with both hands."
—Nigerian Proverb

I was home two days before I even looked at myself. Afraid to see a gaping hole where my breast used to be, I couldn't bring myself to peek.

"Okay, Jo. I hate to do this, but you stink. We need to do something about that," said Paige. I knew she was trying to be funny, but I was in no mood. I wasn't in terrible pain, but I felt so weak.

"I can't shower! I can barely move!" I said. Paige didn't even blink at the tone of my voice.

"Yes, you can. They gave me this post-operative care information packet so I could help you," she said. "Can you stand, do you think?"

I closed my eyes against the bright light that Paige had invited into my bedroom. The blinds had been shut tight for days, keeping the outside world right where I wanted it. I hadn't been ready to face the reality of the new me.

"I'm sorry…I'll try. But don't be a hard-ass. Since when did you get so bossy, anyway?" I said with a grin.

"One step at a time," said Paige, as she pulled back the covers so she could help me. "There, now, just sit on the edge there while I start the water…hang on to that…Okay, now just let your body get some balance back."

With Paige's help, I made it to the bathroom. It felt nice to lean on someone. Slowly, while sitting on the toilet, I unbuttoned my pajama top, averting my eyes from the tubes that clearly ran down my chest. They told me about the tube, inserted to drain away the lymphatic fluid. After my top was off, without looking down, I ran my hands over my chest. My pulse quickened. Even though I knew it was gone, I wasn't prepared for how it would feel, with nothing there. Paige stood quietly, unobtrusive, her eyes locked with mine.

"It's really gone," I said. "How does it look…tell me the truth. Is it hideous?"

"Jo, your breast is gone. But you're still here," she said. I was shocked that Paige was taking it so well. "Take a look. You gotta look sometime. It's not as bad as you think. There's really not a lot of swelling or anything."

Slowly, I stood before the mirror, my hand held tight to the sink. There was a pink line, the incision that went across my chest and under my arm. Little staples were holding it all together. Paige was right; it wasn't really red or swollen. The drain tube was sticking out of my chest, held in place with a couple of sutures. The thing that shocked me the most was not the flatness of my chest, but the way it looked without a nipple. It was weird. It just didn't even look like me.

"I might have them just take the other one off, too. Look how huge it looks now!" I said, holding my heavy breast in my hand. "I thought I had done all my research on this, I thought I was so prepared. But, it's just…so different when it's you. I mean, I knew what it would look like…but, it just feels so strange with…it gone."

I was never one to be shy about my body, so Paige had seen me naked more than once. The first time was when I was folding laundry on a sweltering summer day. I had just finished working out on the treadmill, and I remembered a load of laundry I wanted to fold. Stripped down to nothing, I was sitting on the living room carpet when she walked in looking for a cup of rice. To say she was shocked would be an understatement. She almost looked frightened, and that made me laugh. "Do I look that bad? Jesus, close your mouth. Didn't your mother ever tell you it was rude to stare?" I said with a smirk. She turned her back quickly and I threw a towel around my naked body.

"You're the first to preview the new me," I said to Paige. "Tom hasn't even asked to see it. He's been so helpful these past two days, but he hasn't uttered one word about the surgery. I think he's freaked out, but at least he's here." Paige helped me take off the rest of my pajamas and ease my tired body under the warm cascade of water. It felt so good. Together, we managed to successfully accomplish the shower, new pajamas, and fresh sheets for the bed. I hated to stand by and watch Paige tug at my old sheets, trying to stretch them to fit the bed.

"Thanks. I feel a lot better." And I did. Washing away the stench of the hospital almost made me feel whole again. "Where are Tom and Christopher, anyway?"

"Tom took him out to see Santa Claus at the mall. Can you believe that they're already set up for Christmas at the stores?" said Paige. I didn't really want to think about the holidays.

Thanksgiving was a few days away, and I could care less. Judith had called just after I arrived home and insisted on coming and taking care of Christmas for all of us. A sweet gesture, I know, but having just spent a week with her, I didn't relish the idea of butting heads with her again for a while. She was sympathetic to my plight, but she quickly turned it into a new project for herself. Judith loved to be the heroine and certainly saw my cancer diagnosis and surgery as a way to come and save the day.

"So, what are you doing for the holidays?" I asked Paige. She set down the teapot on the nightstand, and climbed into bed beside me.

"Jason's family is coming this year. I love his mom, so I am so excited to see them all again. It's been three years since we last got together. His dad had knee surgery, and then they went on a three-month cruise. They are so cool." Paige barely talked about her own family. Her mom passed away a long while ago, and she didn't even know where her dad was or if he was alive. Jason's family had always been her surrogate family, she said.

"That's great." A wave of nausea swept over me, and suddenly I felt like I would faint. "I think I'm gonna get some rest before they get home."

Paige didn't answer. She got up from the bed, closed the blinds and slid back in behind me. Her warm body was a comfort; the chill had begun to trickle down my spine again. It came in waves—probably from the anesthetic. When she began to rub my back, first in small circles, then larger ones, I felt sleep start to overtake me. Was this what it was like in the end? When you died, did it just feel like you were drifting into an eternal rest? Death was on my mind a lot these past few weeks.

"Tell me something," I told Paige, my voice slow and quiet. "Tell me something new."

"Something new...hmmm...don't you know everything about me yet?"

"I don't know. There must be something. Tell me about your tenth birthday? Or your first kiss...tell me something new."

Paige stopped circling and wrapped her right arm around me, giving me a gentle squeeze. "Okay, let's see...something nice, though. My first kiss? That would be Joey Sharp. I was in the sixth grade and he told me to meet him out behind the school. So I did. I remember that my heart was racing. He was the cutest boy in Mr. White's class—big brown eyes and shiny dark hair. He had that Donny Osmond smile and all the girls were gaga about him, and he knew it. I didn't think he even gave me a second look, until that day," Paige said. She sat up then, with the pillow behind her back. "So, anyway, I hurried out to the back of the school after the bell rang, and there he was. Even at eleven years old, I knew he was going to break some hearts. I was the only girl in our class who was the same height as him, so maybe that was why he picked me for his secret behind-the-school rendezvous. My heart was pounding, and he put both his arms around my neck...you know, like in a slow-dance position...and went in for the big kiss. I closed my eyes, like I'd seen on an episode of *General Hospital* one day when I was home with the stomach flu. His lips were dry, and kinda cracked, but at that moment I thought it was the best kiss in the whole world."

I smiled. "Then, what?" I asked. "Was that it?"

"No, the next day, I was the talk of the school. It was horrible. I got to school and my best friend told me that he was spreading this vicious rumor about me...already," she said. I could hear her smile. I didn't even have to see her; I could hear it in her voice.

"What was it? Did you grab his crotch or what?"

"No! God, I was just eleven. You're sick! No, he told everyone in our class that I French kissed!" said Paige. "Can you believe it? I didn't even know what it was...French kissing...and here I was being accused of being a French kisser. None of the kids really knew either, but they acted like I had done this horrible thing. They sided with him. It was a nightmare. I spent the whole semester traumatized by that kiss. When I got older and found out the truth, I was so pissed."

"You little slut, you. I always knew you had it in you." I must have fallen asleep then, because I don't remember Paige leaving. When I woke up, I tried to remember my dream. If I write it down right away, I can usually remember, but it was gone. I vaguely remember that Paige and I were together, and it was raining, and she was holding the umbrella. She was trying so hard to keep the umbrella over my head, and the wind kept blowing it away.

***

It was my first day of chemotherapy. Tom was back at work, and Mrs. Stewart had offered to watch Christopher. She had turned out to be the neighbor of my dreams since the surgery. On the first day that I was home from the hospital, she brought over dinner for us. I wasn't eating much, but I knew that Tom was useless in the kitchen, so it was a great help. Then she told me she had asked her church to help out by doing a sort of meal circle. All these people, strangers to us, brought food to our house that first week. It was amazing. I don't think I ever even gave the woman a Christmas card in the few years we had lived in our house.

"How are you doing today, Jo?" Paige asked, as she helped me on with my winter coat. I still could not raise my arms without excruciating pain. The doctor gave me a page of exercises to do to stretch the muscles or some bullshit, but I kept forgetting to do them, opting for the drug-induced sleep instead.

"You know what, from what I've read about this chemo stuff, I'm scared shitless," I told her. I knew that they needed to do the chemo to make sure they cut out all those black cancer cells, but the thought of being sick, nauseated, and weak again frustrated me. I had just started feeling good. I was able to drive without too much discomfort, fold clothes—almost everything I could do before. Now, about to face this, I was irritated.

"How often do you have to go?"

"Once a week, for four weeks, then there's this recovery period—then another...and so on." God, how I dreaded it. "When I read about the side effects, I was not encouraged. It's kind of like one of those lame commercials for diet pills, you know, 'Take Dermathin to lose twenty pounds in one week—side effects may include loss of memory, brain aneurysms, anal leakage, paralysis and more...' But in the case of chemo, there's no small print. It's right there in black and white. Hair loss, loss of appetite, nausea and vomiting, fatigue, and temporary or permanent changes in menstrual cycle. Sounds fun, huh?"

Paige had obviously done her homework, too. "Oh, and don't forget this...I read that many women who receive chemotherapy for breast cancer will experience 'chemo brain.'" She smiled, knowing I would have to ask what the hell that was.

"Chemo brain? Great...and what's that?"

"It's good news, actually. It said that you could suffer from a slight decrease in mental functioning, causing you to forget things. So, you won't even remember the diarrhea and the barfing...cool huh?"

I had to laugh. A decrease in mental functioning was just what I needed.

***

Chemo didn't look like anything at all. It was not what I expected. I was led to a room where there was a row of lounge chairs, coupled with intravenous poles that stood tall waiting for their next victims. The drugs that were intended to kill any stray cancer cells that might be lurking in my body came in clear plastic bags, labeled clearly with my name. The silvery liquid floated there in the bag, looking as harmless as water yet so hazardous that the nurse who carried it to the intravenous pole had to wear heavy-duty latex gloves just to handle it. And this was going to course through my veins? The liquid was labeled in definitive font: "Hazardous Materials" were about to penetrate my bloodstream, conquering the demon cancer that was attacking me. It was a scary thought. *Things labeled* hazardous *really don't belong* in *your body!* There were three different bags, with three separate drugs in them.

"If we use a combination of drugs at a lower dosage, rather than a higher dose of one particular drug, we minimize the side effects," he told me. "It seems to be more effective for breast cancer patients, in recent studies. The therapy we will be using is called CMF; it includes three separate drugs, cytoxan, methotrexate and fluorouracil. You don't have to remember the names, it's just clinical mumbo jumbo." I trusted this man with my life, so I was not about to question his drug of choice, but it felt good knowing what it was they were going to put into my body. I felt confident that he knew what he was doing. Besides, I had searched the Internet and read all I could about all the drugs, and none of them came with any magical "no side-effect" guarantee. In not so many words, it indicated that the cure was worse than the disease. But I wanted all of it out of my body. I had things to do, a child to raise. This was not my time. I hadn't finished my list yet.

The nurse inserted the tubing into the bag and the liquid poison started to drip immediately, making its way toward my bloodstream. It would take a total of two hours to complete the treatment, so I started writing. I would continue to write, each time I came to therapy, and it would turn out to be an inherent part of my early recovery, weaving together the healing of my body with the restoration of my soul.

Seventeen

"I always felt that the great high privilege, relief and comfort of friendship was that one had to explain nothing."
—Katherine Mansfield

Judith arrived right on schedule, arms loaded down with gifts, food, and books. *She really does mean well.* Apparently she thought I hadn't read enough about breast cancer in the past few months and needed to stock my nightstand with the latest. I would have preferred some steamy sex novel, a throbbing hunk of man on the cover with hair down to his shoulders, but the books she brought would certainly not keep me up at night. And after all, I did need my rest.

"Well, you look just wonderful!" she exclaimed, after dropping the load on the living room floor. I looked like shit, and she knew it, but it was nice of her to say. It was actually the nicest thing she had *ever* said to me in my entire adult life. When she hugged me, she held on a little longer than usual. I was accustomed to a peck on the cheek, or the obligatory squeeze, since she was always afraid to mess up her new outfit. This hug was different.

"Thanks, Judith," I said. "I actually feel pretty good today." I tried to schedule all my chemotherapy sessions for Mondays, so that I was well by the weekend. The nausea and the fatigue put me on my ass for about a day, and then it wasn't so bad. I wasn't feeling wonderful, but I was doing okay.

By the time we sorted through all the stuff she brought, I was tired again. The level of energy expelled over the littlest task was incredible.

"There's my favorite boy!" she yelped when Christopher ran into the room. Her hair bounced up and down, all in one piece. She had teased it so high that it looked like a rat's nest when she bobbed around. I had to suppress the urge to laugh as she swung Christopher around. It was hard to believe that so much had changed since she was last here, which was just short of two months ago. I had finished four weeks of chemo already; even that was hard to fathom. Once a week I would drive myself to the hospital, while Paige watched Christopher, and line up with the other cancer patients—who were either bald or balding—and get my infusion of drugs. At first, the only thing that bothered me was the loss of appetite. Everything tasted like metal because of the chemicals coursing through my system. I lost weight quickly, which wasn't so bad, but I was starting to look like a scarecrow.

"How much longer?" Judith asked. I caught her staring at my face. Was it the black circles under my eyes that concerned her, or was she just waiting for me to keel over and die? I hated the way she looked at me, the way so many people looked at me. It was probably what I hated the most. *I don't want to be different; I just want to be me again. Damn it!*

"Three more months and I'm done. Thank the Lord."

"Well, I hope you got a second opinion. I mean, really, they took off your breast; surely they got it all. I don't see the point of chemotherapy, when it's—gone." Judith stood there, her hands on her thin hips. "I can't believe you let them do that—I would never—" Clearly, she was having a hard time with the word *breast.* I doubt she had ever used the word before in her life. "I mean, come on, there's no history of it in our family. Are you sure the doctor wasn't some quack right out of med school looking for a guinea pig to work on?"

Here we go, Judith to the rescue. "That's what it was...Jesus, I wish I was smart enough to figure it out! They always take off women's breasts in the first year of their residency, for practice. I was so lucky that they picked me!" I sat down, exhausted. "For God's sake, Judith, do you think I am a fucking idiot? Do you think I would go through all this—oh, forget it!" I had to leave the room to compose myself, and

I didn't want her to see how out of breath I was, yet another side effect to the chemo.

***

Christmas was not as bad as I thought it would be. Paige and Jason came over for Christmas Eve and I felt pretty good. Judith had calmed down and we managed to have a decent discussion about the fact that my cancer was real. She pushed every one of my buttons whenever we were together, just as she's been doing ever since we were children, but I still love her. You know what they say about picking your family. Never in a million years would I have chosen Judith. But then, I wouldn't have any family left without her. I was feeling the tug of the holiday spirit and tried to see her in a new light. *New beginnings.*

"Jo, I know she bugs you, but you have to realize that the two of you are just so different," Paige said. "And she's scared she's going to lose you, so she's in denial of the whole thing. What better way to deal with it than to make it a doctor's error? That wraps it up for her, nice and neat. Try to see it from her side. She loves you and she's scared. I know how that feels."

Oh, you're so smart, Paige. And so I did try to see it from her side, and Paige was right. Judith was the kind of woman who lived on the outside of everything. Too afraid to dig deep into her own emotional bucket, she kept herself from believing that anything bad could ever happen to anyone she loved. Life was supposed to be casual, all about the best shoes or a reservation at the hottest restaurant in town. For Judith, this was beyond heavy. Denial was easy. Reality sucked.

"Merry Christmas!" I shouted when our guests arrived. The house was warm. The smell of roasted turkey and hot apple pie filled the air. I was so happy that I was well enough to make the dinner. It was my Christmas present to myself. Wellness. Strength and hope for a new year.

The mood was light and festive and I was as happy as I could remember being in a long time. "Isn't it wonderful?" I said to Paige, as I twirled in a circle. She came close to me, gave me a peck on the cheek, and handed me a large oddly shaped package.

"I thought we said we weren't buying for each other this year. I mean, you can't afford it with all those bills for your baby-making doc, and with my bills...well, we won't go there today."

I could see Paige's eyes start to pool. "It's just a little something I found."

Inside was a plant, a large and cascading ivy plant potted in a beautiful ceramic hanging pot. Tears immediately sprung to my eyes. "You remembered that silly book, didn't you?" Ivy was the symbol of friendship and immortality. We had read it in a book a while ago, long before my diagnosis. I had a weird "deja vu" moment of that day I came home from the hospital after Christopher was born. *You rescued me again, Paige.* Paige smiled. "Don't get all mushy," she said. "What did Tom get you this year?" Tom always bought me something really cool. This year he bought me a wonderful writing set, with special books, journals, and a fountain pen. For a guy who doesn't talk much, he does pay attention. I was thrilled that he picked up on my newfound hobby. I'd scribbled a lot in my journals the past month, capturing all the glorious events of chemotherapy on paper. Maybe I would burn it all one day in a huge celebration of the end of it. For now, it kept me sane, gave me a way to let go of it and move on.

I told Paige about the writing supplies and she was surprised. "How come I didn't know you were writing again?"

I used to write for the school paper when I was in college and I loved it, but I hadn't picked up a pen since. "I don't know, I guess I didn't think it was a big deal. It's just a bunch of scribbles, anyway. I always wanted to write, and so this is something I can tick off my list. How about you, what's new?" It seemed that all we talked about anymore was me and I was extremely bored with the subject.

Paige sighed. "Nothing new. We went in to talk about the different types of procedures and are scheduled for our first one in the new year. Everything comes to a dead halt at Christmas. They're talking about boosting my eggs, which sounds weird. Whatever it is, it has something to do with making me more fertile."

Paige had struggled for so long to try to have a baby, and I had no idea how that felt. When Tom and I wanted to make a baby, we just did. One month off the pill and Christopher was conceived. We joked about it back then, how fertile we were, not realizing it wasn't that easy for everyone. My pregnancy was uneventful, just the usual complaints and the added baggage around my ass. I was always slim before I was pregnant, but I quickly got used to my new, shapely body. The full breasts were a huge bonus, too. I felt so sexy with them, and Tom sure enjoyed them, too.

"That's great news," I told her. "And I'm so glad you're seeing one of the specialists. What is it, *in vitro* or something?" Paige explained that they'd go through IUI—intrauterine something or other—but she wasn't sure of the details.

"I saw something about that! Isn't that where they get a turkey baster and inject it up the wazoo?"

Paige nearly choked on the eggnog that Judith had carefully prepared from a recipe that she swore came from Martha Stewart. "Yeah, that's about it, Jo, and thanks for giving me *that* picture. Speaking of turkey," she added. "Is it done? It smells incredible."

***

The holidays had been wonderful, much better than I'd anticipated. When Judith finally left, Tom and I were able to share an evening together, something we hadn't done in a long time. Maybe it was the aura of peace that surrounds Christmas, but he seemed almost at ease around me for the first time since my surgery. It was also the first time in a long time that I didn't feel like a stranger to him. Snow had fallen all night long. On the morning of New Year's Eve I was startled by the sound of the snowplow sputtering loudly down our narrow street. Blurry-eyed, I pulled back the sheer curtains on the bedroom window and saw Paige standing on her front lawn and wearing a snowsuit! *What the hell?* I had never seen the girl in anything that resembled snow gear; a snowsuit was the last thing I'd ever dream of her wearing. I left Tom snoring and threw on some sweats, grabbed a pair of his work boots and a heavy coat, and stumbled outside into the brisk morning air. I almost fell on my ass—the front porch was covered in a powdery, slippery coating of fresh snow.

I skated across the street and snuck up behind Paige as she leaned toward the ground. "Hey!" I yelled as Paige just about toppled over.

"Jesus! What are you doing!" she screeched, regaining her balance by grabbing at my coat. "Are you crazy?"

I spoke through laughter, "The question is, what the hell are *you* doing?" I noticed a large white ball of snow at her feet, and another one that had cut a path through the clean snow.

"I'm building a snowman, what do you *think* I am doing?" she said, holding her chest. "You scared the shit out of me. I could've had a heart attack."

"Nah, you won't have a heart attack. You'll die slowly, making everyone around you suffer endlessly...slowly...sucking every last ..."

"You're a funny, funny girl." She smiled and tossed a handful of snow at me.

I was almost speechless. Paige rarely even went to her car unless someone warmed it up for her, and here she was building a snowman at six-thirty in the morning on a Saturday! Had to be a full moon or something. "So? What's the deal? Are you on those fertility drugs or something? Is this some weird reaction?"

Paige shrugged. "I couldn't sleep. As I was lying in bed watching the snow float past my window, I thought about Christopher, so I thought that if I built a snowman while the snow was wet, he could see it when he got up. I was going to surprise you, call you and tell you to bring him to the window."

I felt a chill run down my spine. To have a friend who loves your child is an awesome thing. Never in a million years could I have found a greater friend than Paige. I would die without her. "You're a good friend."

"It was just a thought," she said quietly. I felt tears come to my eyes.

"Hey," said Paige. "Don't you start crying and ruin my snowman."

Weepiness seemed to be yet another weird reaction to my therapy. I shook it off and said, "Hey, let me do the head part. I have this really cool hat in the house. Got it at the Mardi Gras one year. It's like a conehead hat made out of these cool purple and red and yellow patches. You ever go to Mardi Gras?"

Paige just stared at me. "The wildest place I've ever gone is Chuck E. Cheese's, and that sucked."

"Girl, we gotta do something crazy, you and me!" I rolled the larger ball of snow along the ground. "After this chemo shit is over and I feel semi-normal again, we are going sky diving!" It was on my list. *Sky diving, camping on the beach, running naked into the ocean, going to my son's high school graduation—so many things left to do.*

Paige squinted at me as the snowflakes started coming down harder. "Tell me how we went from Chuck E. Cheese's to sky-diving?"

"Okay, so what would *you* say is crazy for you? And don't say something dumb, like wearing no underpants for a day: been there, done that! Not that exciting, trust me."

I couldn't tell if Paige was blushing or was just cold. Her cheeks turned a rosy shade of red. She was such an easy target: the girl blushed when we talked about tampons! Over the years, though, she'd mellowed a little and it was getting harder to shock her. Inside Paige was a wild woman dying to get out and run naked down the street.

"If you want to know," said Paige. "The most daring thing I want to do is drive on the freeway. I know it sounds ridiculous, but the on- and off-ramps terrify me! I'll go ten miles out of my way to avoid merging with all those crazy drivers. Stupid, huh?"

"No, it's not stupid. We all have those little quirky things," I told her. "I'll teach you and you'll earn your wings."

"There, it's done." The snowman was complete.

One more thing off my list: build a snowman with someone you love.

Eighteen

"Every one of us gets through the tough times because somebody is there, standing in the gap to close it for us."
—Oprah Winfrey

If there was one thing about cancer that I was hoping to skip, it was the hair loss. But I guess it wasn't in the cards. I think I experienced every single damn side effect listed on the now-crumpled pamphlet that the nurse's aide gave me that first day. Nausea, diarrhea, anemia, excessive bruising—the list went on. "Reminds me of those friggin' commercials for hair-growth drugs," I said to Paige as she read it over. "You know the one, where at the end of the commercial the guy talks at hyper-speed, saying 'Side-effects caused by this miracle drug include but are not limited to diarrhea, vomiting, blindness, impotence, paralysis, etc.' But, hey, ya got hair now! The lesser of two evils—die from cancer, or shit myself twice daily. Hmm, let's go with the shitting." Paige didn't smile. In fact, her face was without expression as she continued to read all the horrific things that I might endure to get well.

"Snap out of it! Geez, don't worry, I'm not going to ask you to wipe my ass." I really needed to lighten the mood. "Paige? Earth to Paige. Hey, they just write all that shit so you don't sue them when you get a stomach ache after the chemo. It's legal bullshit, that's all. The doc told me that, with the low doses, I shouldn't feel too much of anything."

Boy, was that doctor wrong! I stared into the mirror at my new self;

the post-cancer reflection seemed to change daily. My face was thinner and it seemed that my skin had become darker. I ran my fingers through my already-thin hair and cringed. I wasn't blessed with Paige's thick locks and the graying brunette hair I did have was painfully sparse. Cut into a bob before the surgery, it now looked ragged. I hated the thought of being bald, but I hated the balding look even more. I was starting to look like Mr. Stewart, next door.

***

I walked right in, like I always did. I can't remember the last time I knocked on Paige's door. Tom always knocked if he was with me and thought I was obscene for just waltzing into her house like I owned it. It was just second nature to me. We dropped the formality of knocking a long time ago. Paige was home to me, so why would I knock?

"Hey, you down there!" I shouted down the stairs to the basement. I heard shuffling and then Paige emerged at the bottom of the steps, rubber gloves on her hands.

"Come on down. I'm finishing up with Mrs. Stewart."

I trudged down the eleven steps and entered her work area. "Well, hello there, Doris," I greeted Mrs. Stewart. Since she had been keeping Christopher so much, she insisted I call her by her first name. Doris had even gone out and picked up a bunch of toddler toys so Christopher wouldn't feel funny about being away from me. I don't know what I would have done without her. It's amazing to me how much kindness people can show to others. Getting to know Mrs. Stewart had been a definite benefit of the cancer. "Where is my little sweetheart?" she asked when she noticed I was alone.

I plopped myself down in the chair with the big dome dryer. It was the most comfortable one in the shop. The others were those fancy wicker-style bamboo-ish things that gave you splinters if you moved your thigh this way or that. "He's gone to a birthday party," I told her. "I was going to go, but I was feeling a little woozy. Must've been the twelve margaritas I had for lunch!"

Mrs. Stewart smiled, her cheeks rosy and her eyes glistening. My angel in disguise. "How are you doing, dear? You look so tired. Can I fix your dinner tonight? I have a canned ham that we can throw some hash browns with—it's not much, but it'll fuel you."

My mouth curled in a grin. I dared not look at Paige, for fear I would laugh out loud. Dear Mrs. Stewart and her wild dinners. The best one yet had been the corned beef hash she brought over, accompanied by boiled potatoes and mashed peas. Lucky for me, I feigned nausea and was off the hook. The first thing I'm going to do when I get well is to buy Mrs. Stewart a cookbook. "No thanks," I told her. "We're fine. I think we're going to have soup tonight. Something light and easy on the stomach." I winked at Paige, who was rolling Mrs. Stewart's gray hair in large pink rollers and anchoring them with long pins. "So, whatcha doing with your hair?" I asked.

"Ah, Paige says I need to curl it up a bit to give my face a lift," said Mrs. Stewart. "Cheaper than a regular face-lift, I suppose, so I told her to have a go at it." She giggled a little, like a schoolgirl. I guess it was always nice having your hair done, no matter what age you were. The feel of the hairdresser's fingers as she roughly massages your scalp is just amazing. It's almost erotic, if you think about it. *And if you have hair.*

"There, now," chimed Paige. "Under the dryer for eight minutes and we'll see the new you." She seemed very bouncy today. "Out you go, Jo." She scooted me out of the comfy dryer chair so Mrs. Stewart could sit down. Paige set the dial on the base of the chair, popped the dome over her client's head and the soft hum of the dryer filled the room.

"So, what's new with you? You look like a girl with a secret to tell," I said. Paige had a sly look on her face. She was never one to keep secrets; I could always tell when she was busting to tell me something. That was the one thing we had in common, we both loved telling secrets. Although I sensed that Paige kept a few more than I did.

"I go in for my insemination tomorrow morning! Can you believe it? I am so excited! They say there's a good chance it could work." Her blue eyes sparkled like a kid who just discovered a shiny quarter from the tooth fairy under his pillow.

She'd waited so long for this; I prayed it would work. "Oh, my God!

When will you know?"

"They said I go in for blood work about a month later."

"Wow, that's great. I guess you're both excited?" I asked, unsure of the response.

Paige nodded furiously. "Jay's nervous about the whole thing, with the sperm samples and all that, but he's excited that we're finally doing something."

I gave her a big hug. "I can't wait for Christopher to have a playmate! Too many old geezers in this neighborhood and not one kid." I looked over at Mrs. Stewart—I had forgotten she was even there. *Oops.* Her eyes were closed; the combination of the whirring sound and the heat had knocked her out.

"I'm trying not to get too excited," said Paige. "The doctor said to relax today. We don't want to scramble any of those precious eggs."

A wave of nausea swept over me and I took a deep breath, which usually helped to control it. "Are you busy right now?" I blurted out. "I'd like you to shave my head."

Paige stared at me like I'd gone mad. "I want you to shave my head." I repeated, sliding into the chair.

"Uh, let me finish up with Mrs. Stewart," Paige said. "And then we can—" Before she could finish the sentence, Mrs. Stewart popped up, fully awake and startled. I think she forgot where she was for a minute. "All done, Mrs. Stewart. Come on over and let's see how you look."

Paige primped and fussed with the woman's curly locks. She sprayed what looked like an entire can of heavy-duty hairspray on her head and our neighbor was set to go. "Mr. Stewart better be taking you out on the town tonight!" I told her. "Because you look absolutely beautiful."

She looked at herself in the mirror, turning her head for a full look, her cheeks flushed at my remark.

"Oh dear, where should we go? It's been so long since we've been out, I wouldn't even know where." The woman pulled the camel-colored winter smock over her pink sweater and wrapped her head in a silk scarf, no doubt to protect the masterpiece.

"Well, now," I told her. "The Silver Lantern, just outside the city, is the place. So you go home, hide the TV remote, and tell Mr. Stewart that if he wants supper tonight, it's The Silver Lantern or nothing! You look fabulous, dahling, just fabulous!"

She blushed again and then headed up the stairs, a new bounce in her step. That was the one thing about Paige's job that must be so great, seeing the results of her work in the smiles of her customers, knowing she'd made them feel a little better about themselves, if only for a while.

"Bye, ladies," said Mrs. Stewart. "You behave now, ya hear! See you soon!" Her voice carried like a melody back down the stairs.

"God, she is one sweet woman," I said, when I heard the front door close. "I bet she was a hoot in her day, the life of the party."

Paige busied herself with clearing the rollers, pins, and brushes. "Yeah, she is a sweetheart." Without turning to me, she asked, "Josie, do you miss having a mom? Mrs. Stewart, I'll bet she's a great mom." Paige got a little funky when we talked about our parents, and I needed her to be fully aware so she could shave my head.

"Not to change the subject," I said. "But I'm serious about this: I really do want you to shave my head."

Paige stood behind me, stared past me into the mirror as she talked to my reflection. "I don't think I can."

"Just look at my hair, it's turning to crap. I'd rather wear some hip new scarf than walk around like this. It's getting obscene...look!" I lifted a tuft of hair to reveal a spot where you could count the number of hairs.

"It'll grow back. Remember what they said?"

"Look, either you shave it or I will; I just don't want to cut off my ear. Please. Then we can go online to that cool place where they make those hats with hair. What do ya think? Come on," I begged. I hated to plead, but this was one thing I wasn't going to back down on.

"Okay, okay. Geez, you are impossible! What if you have an ugly head? Don't cry to me if you have a warped skull." She smiled at me and I settled deeper into the chair.

"I promise," I told her. "You know, *caveat emptor*, let the buyer beware. I won't even yell if it looks ridiculous." I had brought along some scarves I'd just purchased at the Dollar Mart.

Paige shook her head. "*Caveat emptor*, you got that right. I should've have read that disclaimer about our friendship before I signed on. I guess I didn't know what I was in for."

The buzz of the electric razor was the last thing I heard. When I looked up, I was as bald as a new baby.

Nineteen

"I like nonsense; it wakes up the brain cells. Fantasy is a necessary ingredient in living, it's a way of looking at life through the wrong end of a telescope and that enables you to laugh at life's realities."

—Dr. Seuss

It was a sunny day in August, right after Paige discovered, once again, that she wasn't pregnant, when we started talking about planning a getaway—a girls' weekend away. With a little pleading and begging, I convinced her it was time for us to take the long-awaited road trip that we had discussed ever since my diagnosis last year. It was the perfect time of year to go, the summer heat was just starting to envelop the small town, causing its inhabitants to hide under hissing air conditioners all afternoon. There was no fun to be had around here.

Paige was mindlessly organizing the pink rollers in the three-tiered plastic cart when I asked her if she was ready to take off on an adventure. "I don't know," she said, looking up from the mound of foam. "I just can't walk out on my customers. I do work, you know. I don't know. Where would we go, anyway? What would you do with Christopher? What about Jason...who would be here for him? I just can't take off at the drop of a hat." She was trying to convince herself to be responsible—or she was once again hearing the nagging of her uptight husband. "I just don't know what you see in her—the two of you are so…so…opposite," I had overheard him say one evening when I stepped into the front entrance to holler for her to come see the sun setting behind her house. Jason had always disapproved of me, though for the life of me I couldn't figure out why. There was just something about me that irritated him. Paige said he just didn't understand me the way that she did. Was I *that* hard to understand? Okay, a small part of me delighted in the fact that Paige's husband found me so dangerous, such a bad influence on his precious wife. Even in my fragile state, after being pumped with toxic chemicals, Jason still observed me as a genuine threat.

"You know, your husband is a big boy, Paige. He can make his own dinner and put on his own clothes for one damn day! Don't get me started…" I turned to walk up the stairs. "I'm heading out to the spa—it's time to de-fur the legs. I have Hilda booked for both of us at two if you wanna join me." I watched as Paige's mouth curled slightly and a smile began to form at the edges.

"Oh my God! You are going to let the Amazon woman wax you again?" yelped Paige.

"They didn't have anyone else and my legs have been in hibernation for the past few months," I said. "Besides, with the amount of hair growth on my legs, I am going to need Hilda's huge arms to yank it all out! I haven't shaved in God knows how long and you don't even want me to tell you about my bikini line…it's pathetic. Does the name Sasquatch mean anything to you? I think he may be a distant cousin." With that, Paige was convinced. Apparently, the idea that she might be able to share in my pain was just what she needed to sway her.

"All right…I'll go. I mean, I'll ask Jay. He might have plans or something."

My heart began to beat again in normal rhythm. I didn't know how much I really wanted this trip until I thought she might not go for it. The past year had been a drain on both of us—on all of us. Christopher was finally getting back a shell of the woman he once knew as his mother, a little thinner in both body and spirit sometimes. My hair was back—well, it was almost back. When it returned, it was darker, with more gray, and the texture was finer than it had been before I had it shaved off.

Paige still bugged me about that. During those months when it was thinning, falling out in huge grotesque patches, I couldn't take it. After Paige shaved it, I had so much fun dressing up my bald head. I found this wonderful place online that made hats with hair and made fast friends with the owner, who supplied me with several cute hats. One was a baseball cap with a cute brunette ponytail and another was a beachy hat with slightly shorter, highlighted wisps of soft tresses peeking out under the straw. The woman was amazing. Having survived cancer, the treatments, and all the stresses of recovery, she designed these spectacular creations to encourage others, like me, to experiment with our newfound baldness, to think of it as an adventure. And I did just that. Depending on what mood struck me, I could be a new woman every day. Paige thought it was hilarious, and my neighbors barely knew me when I strolled the sidewalks at the first hint of spring. They were probably wondering who the hell the skinny tart was with the blonde Shirley Temple locks. I enjoyed every minute of the confusion I caused the sleepy neighborhood.

***

The salon was located on the lower level at the strip mall just around the corner from my house. A fairly new business, its ultimate goal was to bring the residents of Maple Grove, Iowa, into the twenty-first century. The building was situated on the corner, across from Sudsy's Laundromat, and housed a legal firm, a tooth whitening clinic, a pet food shop and a Thai restaurant that had just opened not more than three months ago. The spa was in a weird location—an elevator on the far side of the building took you down to the dark hallway that led to its doors. In the whole plaza, it was the only business that seemed to be in the depths of the earth. Upon entering the spa, you were greeted (almost assaulted) by a perky twenty-ish employee with perfectly coifed hair and weapon-like fingernails. The lighting was soft, diffused by beautiful parchment lampshades. The furniture was elegant, floral designs in warm, tranquil tones that set the mood for the treatments they provided.

***

"The only thing that has escaped at that spa was a hundred bucks: escaped right from my wallet!" Paige had said when I tried to entice her to a day of pampering not long after her second IUI treatment.

True, it was costly, but sometimes you had to pay the price for a little relaxation. Paige was getting anxious about the waxing. The memory of our last leg waxing was still fresh in her mind. "I can't believe I'm doing this again!" Paige said in the tiny elevator on the way downstairs. "The last time I had this done, a part of the hot wax was stuck to my inner thigh afterward. Every time I moved, my upper thighs stuck together!"

I laughed. "I know. It's awful, but the razor burn alone will keep me coming back. It just isn't pretty when I shave my legs. A little pain and voila! No hair growth for two to three weeks…it's heaven! Besides, it only hurts for a minute."

We were greeted and seated and awaiting the *Amazon woman* when the bell on the door jingled behind us. I turned to the sound to see a pretty woman in a beautiful red blouse heading our way. "Oh my God! Josie? Is it really you?" the woman yelped. I searched her face for a sign of recognition. Nothing. I had no idea who this woman was. She was on me like spots on a leper before I could get up off the chaise. "You look absolutely…um…thin. How are you? I didn't think…I mean, the ladies at the Ski Club last winter…you know, Susan Blakely right? The woman who had her boobs done last spring? She told me…" The woman blabbered on while I watched her with a furrowed brow.

"Oh, Susan. Yes, she has a little girl my son's age. That Susan?"

The woman smiled. "Yes, I didn't know you knew her…and she didn't know I knew you…so, anyway, how are you?"

It was then that I realized who this absurd woman was. She was a girl I went to high school with a century ago. She had gained a ton of weight and had a nose job or something but it was definitely her. Ditzy Deborah—the girl most likely to count the days until her high school reunion. She enjoyed high school way more than a person had a right to. She belonged to the glee club, cheerleading squad, band, badminton club and God knows what else, just so that she could be in the year book more than anyone at Maple Grove High. Quite the feat—and she pulled it off. Her glowing face could be found on more than forty-eight pages in every one, four years in a row.

"You look great," I said. Even with the extra poundage, she did have a glamorous "air" about her. "I am good." I didn't really know what to say. I hadn't seen the woman for so long, I wasn't sure what I wanted to say. It's not like we were friends.

"Thank-yuuuu!" she replied, squeezing through to sit next to Paige on the sofa. "It's just been years since we saw each other, Josie. How is the cancer thing?" Nothing like approaching it gently. It was obvious she was still the "class gossip" as well as dumb as a doorknob.

"The cancer thing?" I felt my face redden a little and glanced at Paige, who had moved as far to the side as she could on the tiny sofa. "Why, it's just fine. I'm good to go, now."

Deborah's face contorted. "Oh, Susan thought for sure…well, I mean, the ladies were worried that you had…you know, how much time did they give you?"

I swallowed. "Hummm. What was it, Paige? Twenty years? Thirty?"

Deborah shifted. "Oh dear God! I am so sorry. There I go again. I really don't know how I got all that mixed up. I will have to run over there and straighten those ladies out for you, Josie. Those poor ladies had you on your deathbed; can you believe it? I just don't know *how* these things get so twisted up." Deborah had retrieved a pocket mirror from her designer bag and was meticulously applying a fresh coat of Ruby Red to her lips when Hilda lumbered over to announce it was time for Paige's crotch-ripping session.

"So nice to see you, Deborah. Stay well now."

"Yes, thanks. I certainly will. And not to worry, I will set everyone straight." She winked, producing a cell phone and shaking it at me. "Not to worry."

Twenty

"The purpose of a life is a life of purpose."
—Robert Byrne

On the road. All visible hair had been removed from Paige's ankles to her hips and the two of us were on the road to nowhere. I was pumped; Paige was scared shitless. Could be because I encouraged her to get behind the wheel and now she was headed south on I-35, white knuckles wrapped around the steering wheel.

"See, it isn't so bad, now is it? You're doing great," I encouraged her. Her head didn't move; her eyes were glued to the front of the car.

"Don't talk to me. It's distracting."

"Oh, sorry. So, you don't want me to tell you that there's a semi-truck riding your ass, then?" Paige's eyes danced right, checking the mirror for the truck. Her head still didn't move.

"Funny." Though I don't think she was amused. A car zipped past; horn blaring. I looked over at the speedometer and she was idling at about forty-five miles an hour!

"Come on. You might want to try to keep up with traffic," I told her. "Follow a little closer to that car just ahead…Okay, that's it, a little faster. The speed limit here on the highway is actually seventy miles per hour…it's good to keep up or you'll get creamed. Loosen up your grip; relax your shoulders. Jesus, you're going to lock up if you sit like that the whole way."

"The whole way! No...you said just ten minutes. That's it for me." Paige slowed the vehicle, turned slightly to the right and eased it onto the dusty shoulder of the highway. "Fun's over. Thanks. Your turn."

I laughed. "You've been through enough. I'm proud of you—really. You went twenty minutes on a busy freeway. Aren't you so excited? You conquered your fear!"

"As soon as my butt cheeks unclench, then I'll be excited." I was glad she still had her sense of humor. "Hey, thanks. It was kind of fun, really, for a minute. I'm glad you 'forced' me to do it."

"No problem. This weekend is gonna be great, isn't it?" I was so excited to be flying down the highway, windows wide, with the wind blowing my new hair. It felt like the past year never happened. I felt free for the first time in months. "Hey, you want to stop for a coffee? There's an exit about ten miles up the road."

"Coffee would be great. So, how far are we going anyway? Did you actually have a plan?"

I grinned. I actually did have a plan, even though she thought I was aimlessly driving across the state. I discovered long ago that Paige had an obsession with the novel *The Bridges of Madison County*. Paige was a reader. She read anything and everything she could get her hands on. From my living room window, I often caught sight of her sitting on her front porch, book in lap, coffee cup at her side. She always looked so calm, sitting there. On her coffee table at home, a book with all the photos of the bridges was displayed. The main wall in her entrance was adorned with photographs of the six historic bridges that are scattered across the countryside in south-central Iowa. So that was where I was taking her. I couldn't believe that she had never seen the bridges, living a mere forty miles from the birthplace of the author and the home of the bridges.

"Of course I haven't been there. How would I get there?" she had told me one day when we were discussing places we would like to go. Her fear of driving on the busy roads had kept her from realizing a longtime dream—to walk across all six remaining bridges of Madison County.

This weekend, that dream would be fulfilled.

***

"Oh my God!" Paige shrieked upon reading the sign ahead: *Winterset Home to The Bridges Of Madison County*. "Oh my God! Jo! I can't believe it!"

"Cool, huh? Did you know this is where John Wayne was born, too?" This was actually a very interesting place, with lots to see. The six bridges and the boyhood home of the Duke himself were on my mental list of "must-sees."

I pulled into the Super 6 Motel just after 10 a.m. The lot was packed, but I had called ahead to reserve a room for the night. "Is this okay?" I asked Paige, pointing to the Super 6 sign.

"Whatever! I don't care if I sleep in the car. I'm here! I'm really going to see the bridges!" Paige squirmed in the seat, her nose pressed up against the window like a kid seeing Disney World for the first time.

"I never did understand your fascination, but I have to say I am a little excited, too. Be kinda cool to see where they filmed the movie—stand where Eastwood stood while he romanced Meryl Streep, and all that."

"Thanks, Jo. This is just so awesome! I can't wait to see them," said Paige. "I just can't believe you did this…how long…what made you …" Her voice trailed behind me.

"Okay, just get your junk out of the car, would ya?" I said with a laugh. "I know, I'm the best friend in the whole world, you will *never* be able to repay me…hey, that works for me. Always in debt to me… hmmm …I'm likin' it."

The room was decent, with two double beds, a dresser, a desk, two chairs and a tiny bath. Upon quick inspection, I was thrilled to discover it was sparkling clean.

"I have a map for all the locations—where do you want to go first?"

"Let's got to the Roseman Bridge; that's the one where Robert Kincaid stops Francesca to ask for directions and it's where she leaves him that note," says Paige, her voice giddy. "What a romantic story it was, wasn't it?"

"Yeah, but she did fool around on her husband," I reminded her.

It was a beautiful story; the kind every woman took to her dreams after reading it. Who didn't yearn for that kind of longing and romance in their lives?

"I know, but it's like it didn't matter. It's weird."

"So, if some handsome man showed up at your door, swept you off your feet, what would you do?" I asked.

Paige was silent for a few minutes. "I hate to say it, but I think that if a Robert Kincaid-like figure knocked on my door today, I might be tempted."

I was shocked. It was not the answer I expected from her. "God, really! You? I just couldn't see it." Paige looked a little wounded. "I didn't mean that it couldn't happen," I corrected myself. "I just meant that you seem so devoted to Jason, that's all."

"He had an affair," Paige blurted out, quickly turning her head away as she spoke. The words hung in the air for a minute.

"What! He had an affair? What are you talking about?" I said. I just couldn't imagine Paige's husband ever having an affair. And why didn't I know about it? "How? When? Why didn't you...him, really?"

"It was before you and I met. He slept with this tramp from work—some redhead that answered phones back then. He says she came on to him, but I don't know and I didn't care at the time who did what to whom. But, he did...sleep with her. I mean ..." Her voice trailed.

I was flabbergasted. Who in the hell would want to sleep with him anyway—not that I would say that to my friend, but really! The guy oozed of arrogance. He wore his ego on his lapel like fragrant rose. "I can't believe you never told me," I said. "So, what did you do?"

Taking a deep breath, she said, "I forgave him...obviously, but it wasn't easy. There are nights, even now, when we are making love when I wonder. You know, I wonder if he's thinking of her. It was tough in the beginning, but now...not so bad."

I didn't believe her. It was still bad. I could see it in her eyes. "I just can't believe it!" I said loudly. "Sorry, I'm sorry...that must have been so difficult. That's the one thing I can say about Tom—he's as faithful as an old do. Or maybe he's just too lazy to find another woman who will put up with his shit!"

Paige smiled. "The woman quit after she found out I knew about their fling and I really don't know where she is now," said Paige. "I guess Jay doesn't either, but I don't ask. I had to let go of it a long time ago. It was either that or get a divorce. You just can't hang on to it; it will kill you. As it is, it changed us. Something like that has to change a marriage, don't you think?"

"Yeah, I know you can forgive, but can you really forget something like that?" *I know I couldn't.*

Paige shrugged. "You know what? You can forgive, let go of the pain, but no…you never forget a betrayal like that. I'm sure it changed the course of our marriage somehow…it's in the past and that's where I leave it. Too much else to worry about these days."

Paige retreated into silence again until we reached our final destination—Roseman Bridge.

Twenty-one

"Partake of some of life's sweet pleasures. And yes, get comfortable with yourself."
—Oprah Winfrey

After spending the day traipsing all over the countryside, I was ready for a quiet dinner and a good night's sleep. Paige was still high from her journey across the bridges. I took her photo on each bridge, and on the last one, Paige enlisted the help of a nearby sightseer so that we could both get in the picture. At the end of the day the bright smile was still plastered on her face, like a kid who just finished off the last of his cotton candy and was finally content. Paige looked almost peaceful in her glee.

The room was sweltering hot when we returned. We had forgotten to enlist the aid of the window air conditioner and the dry heat of the day filled every crevice. "Shit! It's like a friggin' oven in here!" I said upon being assaulted by the steamy air. Turning the air to a crisp COLD setting, I collapsed on the bed closest to the window and stripped off every stitch of clothing.

Paige seemed in a daze and floated through the room, moving this, rearranging that, until she had exhausted all the adrenaline that was coursing through her veins. "It's a cute room, don't you think? I like it."

"I don't know...if you like floral bedspreads and green shag carpet, it's fine. These are the best hotels really, though—they're clean and friendly—that's all I need when I travel. We usually stay in them whenever we go on the road. Where do you stay?" It suddenly dawned on me that in the years that I had known Paige and Jason, I don't think I had ever seen them go away together.

"Jason hates to travel," Paige announced. "He can't stand the idea of sleeping in a bed that has been used by someone else. He watches too many of those documentaries. He saw one ten years ago where they brought in this special ultra-violet light that detected even the most minute traces of bacteria and the reporters found the hotel room bedding full of all these different kinds of germs. It was the end of his traveling days."

"No shit?" I couldn't believe that he was *that* anal. "Even a fancy hotel? He won't do that? There are some really nice hotels that I am *sure* would be bacteria-free." I almost laughed, but didn't want to insult her. Sometimes we could joke about Jason, but other times I had to be careful what I said. He was her husband after all, and she loved him as is—anal tendencies and all. There is always that fine line with friends—the line is something I have a lot of trouble with some days.

"Nope. No hotels, motels, cottages or cabins for him. He's a stay-at-home kind of guy," she said. "It's fine with me. I don't mind." Her tone was less than convincing.

"So...what shall we do know, chick?" I said, quickly changing the subject.

Paige sat up against the quilted headboard, leg stretched out in front of her. "I don't know about you, but I am starved. Where should we eat?"

On the bedside table rested a booklet, *Restaurant and Lodging Guide.* I flipped through it casually. "What do you feel like? Chinese? Italian?"

"I think I feel like Italian—any in there?" Paige asked, heading toward the bathroom.

"Uh...let's see. There's a couple. One is about a block from here, so we could walk. It's called Casa Mancini. It says 'Casa Mancini serves authentic Italian cuisine, prepared fresh daily. Offering both indoor and outdoor dining experiences, our menu boasts spirited pasta, beef and veal entrees, a variety of seafood dishes and a rotating selection of delectable desserts.' Man, I am hungry now! Let's go!"

"Sounds great!" Paige yelled, though I doubt she heard a word over the sound of the water pelting on the tile. "I'll just be a minute!"

I settled back against the pillow, and fighting sleep I reached for the phone. It rang just twice at the other end when I heard the husky voice of my husband. "Hallo?"

"Hey babe, how are you?" I said. "How's my big boy?"

"The big boy is doing great, and Chris is doing good, too," he said with a laugh. "How you doin'? Where are you now?"

"We're in Winterset. We just spent the day looking at every covered bridge in the area. It was fun," I told him. "What did you two do?" I felt my heart flare a little, mother-guilt pains I'm sure. I hadn't left Christopher for more than a day since he was born. Though I loved to go for long solo drives when I could, I never went anywhere overnight without him. Unless you count my time in the hospital, which I have only vague memory of anyway, due to the serious painkillers I was on. This was my first real journey from home without my boy.

"Ah," said Tom. "We were just sitting down to a healthy dinner of canned spaghetti, then it's off to the park for a little rough-housing. We can do that now 'cause you aren't here!" I laughed. Tom knew how much I hated the wrestling he and Christopher did, thinking him too young for that sort of handling.

"Okay then...give him a big kiss from Mommy. Tell him I miss him and I'll see him before his favorite bunny show comes on tomorrow, okay?"

Tom grunted. "Sure thing. Have fun. We're fine. Bye."

"Bye. I love y..." The sound of a click cut me off. Men! Why in the world did we mix ourselves up with them? Oh, yeah...they helped us make beautiful children.

***

The restaurant was a little darker than I expected and much bigger than it looked from the outside. The walls were a deep shade of terra cotta and there were beautiful flowers, potted plants, and colorful pottery scattered here and there, creating an elegant, yet casual, feel. We were seated in the back corner, against the window in a little alcove. It was early and customers were sparse. The waiter arrived wearing a burgundy vest, white shirt and paisley bow tie. He rambled off all the specialties of the day, including his recommendation for a Merlot that would be "spectacular" with any of the selected menu items. We chose the wine, ordered a couple of Caesar salads, and asked him to hold off on ordering our entrees until we gave him the signal.

"There is *nothing* worse than being rushed out of a restaurant," I declared. "I learned a long time ago that if I wanted to enjoy a peaceful dinner, it was better to stall the order. Don't you just hate getting the bill before your main course?"

"I know what you mean," said Paige. Taking a deep breath, she released the last of the excitement of the day. Her face was still glowing, and her body seemed more relaxed as she slumped a little in the high-backed chair. "Thanks for a fantastic day. I will remember it forever."

"It was purely selfish," I began. "It's that damn list of mine. The next one was 'Take a dear friend to a place she's always wanted to go.' Can't fight the *list*, now can I? I am reaching mid-point and I don't want to fuck with it."

Paige laughed.

The salads were put in front of us and we devoured them in minutes. "Shit, I was hungrier than I thought," I said, setting the bowl to the edge of the scalloped tablecloth. "Must be all this fresh air. It's been so long since I felt well enough to move so much. It's great. How are you doing? Feeling okay?" I knew the meds that the fertility doctor had her on often made her feel nauseated and tired. We were quite the pair.

"Oh yeah, I'm fine. Off all meds for the moment," she said. "Taking a break. My body is tired. I don't know if I want to continue with it. It's been so many months of treatments, probing—we are both burnt out on baby-making in a test tube."

I was shocked. "You aren't going to give up, are you?" I took a swig from the wine glass, my third glass of the red wine that Luciano suggested. It took two and a half glasses before it actually started tasting good. Now the warmth of the alcohol was seeping down my torso to my lower body.

Paige sighed, a tear forming at the corner of her eye. She blinked it away. "Yeah, I hate to admit it but we are thinking of giving up, Jo. I just can't take it anymore. The mood swings, the hot flashes, and the bad sex…it's too much! Our marriage has been reduced to something clinical and it's getting to both of us. I just don't think we can do it anymore. And then there's the expense…you don't even want to know what it's cost us so far…and you know what a tightwad my husband is…"

I reached over and rubbed her hand. "I'm sorry. I wish it were easier for you. It's not fair."

"Yeah, I know, but you should know that better than anyone," Paige said turning to me. "How can you still be so positive and upbeat? How do you do it? I just get so wasted by the stress and you seem to come up with fists swinging, ready for the next fight. God, I wish I had that in me."

Our entrees arrived and the aroma of garlic and pesto filled the air. "Man, that smells so amazing. Don't you wish you could cook like that?" I asked Paige. "One more thing to add to my list—take a decent cooking class. Care to join me in a culinary venture?"

"After today, Jo, I'd follow you just about anywhere," Paige said. "You are one special friend." She bent across the table and wrapped her arm around my neck, kissing me on the cheek.

"Aw shucks…eat your pasta and shut up…don't get all sappy on me or the waiter will think we're lesbians or something." The sound of our mouth-filled giggles drowned out even the violinist who was playing off-key in the room behind us.

***

Back at the hotel room, we each lay on our beds, staring at the white ceiling. "Wonder how much bacteria is on these sheets?" Paige said, giggling at herself. We had polished off the entire bottle of wine at dinner and were both feeling delightfully drunk.

I got up and started to open another bottle that I had stashed in my bag. "So, tell me something I don't know. Can we play that game?" I was surprised that Paige had divulged her husband's indiscretion early that day—usually she was tight-lipped about anything negative in her personal life—always wanting everyone to believe she had it all together. But she never fooled me and she knew it.

Paige sat up slowly. "Sure...okay...something about me you don't know. Let me think," she started. "I hated my father. How's that one?"

"Shit...couldn't you find something *fun* to tell me? Anyway, I think you told me that one already. Your father was just a product of his generation. Everyone hated their father in the seventies." I set two plastic cups filled with wine on the side table between the beds. "Okay, if that's all you've got, then it's up to me."

"Ah, I know *everything* about you," Paige declared. "You have a big mouth, remember?"

I smiled. "Ah, but you don't. Everyone has secrets, Paige. Everyone. Even me."

Paige leaned in closer, afraid she might miss something I was saying. "Shoot."

I settled myself comfortably so that I could watch her reaction. "My biggest secret...this is big, so you can't go blabbing it to fancy-pants," I told her.

Her forehead crinkled. "Who?"

"Your husband...no telling anyone...deal?" I leaned between the beds and shook her hand, just about toppling us both to the shaggy moat below.

"My secret is that I used to work as a topless dancer in New York City."

I watched as Paige's mouth dropped, her eyes widened. It was so entertaining. She was at a loss for words. "Uh...you...no way...you were not...you were a stripper?"

I was sure she would want to run out the door. "Seems kind of ironic now, huh? Me, the topless dancer—now left with only one boob. Guess it was a good thing I quit when I did." I laughed.

"I can't believe it," Paige said, still in shock. "You took off your clothes for dirty old men? That's so wild! Jason would have a fit if he knew that about you!" And he never will, I thought. That's the great thing about having a best friend, sharing secrets.

I glared in her direction. "No…I took off my top for dirty old men. I was really, really young—too young to be working there, actually. I had a fake ID and needed the money," I said. "And no telling anyone! Especially not your husband…Jesus, this would be our first *and* last road trip."

"How in the hell did you go from a New York dancer to an Iowa housewife?"

"It was more like Iowa to New York," I corrected her. "I grew up here, you know that. Then, when I was sixteen, I left home for the big city. I wanted to be a star—maybe I still do. I wanted to write screenplays but I knew that I had to work my way up to it. I thought I could model or land some small acting job or something. I was young and naïve, like all sixteen-year-olds. I found a job in a diner, rented a shitty basement apartment that reeked of cat piss, and thought I had it all. I was on my way."

"Sorry to interrupt, but are you sure this is your life? It sounds vaguely like the movie-of-the-week. Are you shitting me?"

"No…I shit you not!" I said, taking a large swig of the cheap Merlot. "It was really me. I worked in a crappy diner during the day and then this customer told me that they were opening up a nightclub down the block. He asked me if I wanted to make some extra cash, so I danced."

Paige leaned forward, releasing a large burp. "Oops, 'scuse me. So, was it awful?"

"It was pretty awful…not at first…but it got to be weird," I said. "After about eight months I quit and ran home with my tail between my legs. It was too scary. It was then—when I was safely in college—that I met Tom. We don't talk much about my 'dancing' days. Tom knows the whole story, but it was no big deal to him. I think at the time he thought it was kinda sexy. The pervert!"

"Oh my God! Jason would leave me if he found out I was a stripper…sorry, topless dancer," Paige exclaimed. "I still can't believe you didn't tell me. That is a huge secret! So, why didn't you tell me before?" Paige slumped down in the bed, covering herself to the neck with the white sheet.

I shrugged. It was so long ago that it didn't feel so huge anymore. "I don't know...I guess I thought maybe you would think differently of me," I told her. "I mean, you know...think I was some slut or something. I was so young. You do things when you're young that you can't take back. They aren't always things you are proud of; they aren't things that you want to share with everyone, but they are still a part of you. They shape you; form you into the person you are today. You can't be ashamed but you can have regrets. It's the regrets that can hurt so much." Paige looked over at me, her eyes were sad, sadder than I had ever seen them. "It's fine, Paige. Don't be sad for me. I am okay with everything from my past. Now, your turn...what's your deep dark secret? Tell me something really shocking—did you rob a 7-Eleven? Flash a teacher? Come on...you must have a skeleton somewhere in your neatly organized closet."

Paige shifted, her eyes still locked on me. She sat up in the bed and leaned against the headboard. "I gave away my baby girl."

I moved forward, stunned. "Paige...what are you talking about?"

"When I was raped, I got pregnant," Paige said, putting her hand on her tummy. "It was a girl, and I gave her up."

"Oh my God! How awful. Ah, honey, don't cry." I crawled into her bed, took her in my arms like a child, and she shook and shook for I don't know how long. My own words still lingered in the air between us. *It's the regrets that can hurt so much.*

Twenty-two

"It takes a long time to grow an old friend."
—John Leonard

For two friends who thought they knew absolutely everything there was to know about each other, Paige and I discovered over the weekend that there were still many doors unopened. We talked most of the night and I let Paige lead the way. When it came to the rape and her pregnancy, I was unsure as to how to proceed. "It was the worst day of my life," she said, after the tears had dried. "I still remember the look on that nurse's face, so self-righteous, like she was saying, 'You little tramp, you'll remember this beautiful baby's face forever and it serves you right.' She didn't even know how I got pregnant, no one did. When I started to show, I was shipped off to California to stay at my aunt's."

I sat next to Paige, my arm still around her shoulder as she poured out the story. Listening to her, it could've happened last week, every detail was so clear and precise. "Was she nice, your aunt?"

Paige grimaced. "She was worse than my father and reminded me every day that I was going to hell. She read from the Bible every night so that God would cleanse my soul. It was awful, Jo. I sat at the kitchen table while she read one verse after another, getting louder and louder, until she was almost screaming, her arms raised to the heavens. I felt so dirty."

I listened intently as she retold the events and it was like a horrible novel. "I don't know how you got through it," I told her. "It makes me so sad for you. No wonder you hate your parents."

Paige nodded and moved closer. "One day, I was cooking dinner for the two of us—she didn't have any children—and my water broke. I didn't know what had happened. I felt stickiness between my legs and then the cramping started. I was frightened; my aunt was frantic. Instead of helping me, she knelt and prayed while I screamed in pain." Paige went on to describe how she was forced to kneel in front of the cross and pray for her soul, while repeating "Forgive my evil ways and cleanse my body and soul" twelve times before being driven to the hospital. As Paige recalled the intense pain, I noticed she was clutching her stomach.

"My daughter was born forty-five minutes after I arrived," she said. "And then I went home without her two days later. And that was that. Everything went back to normal."

With that, Paige closed her eyes. She didn't wake until morning.

***

The homecoming was not what I expected. Whatever happened to absence making the heart grow fonder? This was more like *absence makes the husband grow uglier.* Tom had fully supported my need to get away, but he sure didn't show it when I arrived at lunch time on Sunday.

"Thank God you're home!" were the first four words out of his mouth when he saw me. No "Hi, honey, I missed you." No hugs at the door, no joyous face at the arrival of his lovely wife, just the usual griping. "Jesus, this kid of yours is a handful! We were doing great until nap time yesterday. How the hell do you get him to sleep? And why in the hell does he take his diaper off, anyway? When did this start?"

The hair on my neck rose to combat position and then retreated, too tired for the battle. "Hi, honey, I'm home," I chimed. "And yes, I missed you too, sweetheart." Then, the patter of tiny feet and my arms were filled with my handsome, blonde-haired boy. As though the moon had come and entered my chest, my heart expanded, leaving little room for the next beat. Life was good again. "There you are, you little monkey,"

I laughed. "Were you causing trouble for Daddy? That's a good boy! Just like we practiced." I looked over at Tom, who had relaxed his stance and was forging a grin of surrender.

"Yeah, we did okay, and I'm glad you are back."

"And yes," he added. "We missed you."

I embraced him, my arms barely reaching around his large chest. Tom had always been husky—not fat, but football player husky. His voice was husky, his body was husky, and he made love like a husky man. Not gentle, but hard and fast, as if rushing for a touchdown. In those days, however, I took what I could get. His once-insatiable appetite for me had been replaced by his worry over my hair loss, my vomiting, and my lack of energy. I think he was afraid to touch me, for fear of hurting me.

I unpacked my clothes, throwing the lot into the washing machine, then settled on the sofa to cuddle with my boys. My mind was full of the secrets Paige and I had revealed, things not even Tom knew. Things he really wouldn't care to know. Insignificant details, like the fact that my first bike was green and that my dad had retrieved it from someone's trash and fixed it up for me. The local lumber store was out of red paint, so he painted it green. And there was my first love. Tom thought that he was my first, but Paige knew that it was Jimmy Gonzales, a kid who moved into our neighborhood when I was eleven. He was dark and dreamy, fifteen years old, and I was so in love with him that I couldn't sleep at night. I heard his voice in my dreams; it was pathetically cute. He moved away three months after he arrived and my heart was broken. He must have thought I was a dumb kid, swooning after him like a puppy. I kept a journal every night. Sometimes I open it and read about my early love affair with a boy who didn't know my name.

***

I tossed and turned that first night home. Awakening at four, I took my new journal out to the front porch and opened it. In the predawn, there was an eerie silence, the only sound being the soft whisper of trees.

August 15, 1999

I don't know how to talk to Paige about the baby. I am so sad for her, especially now. Now that she wants a baby so badly. I can't even imagine that kind of pain—to see your child, and then have to hand it over to strangers.

When I went into Christopher's room tonight, I was struck by how beautiful he is when he's sleeping. His blonde hair is filling in so quickly. His baby face is thinning and I am not ready to declare him a little boy—not yet. I love being a mom. Of everything I've done in my life, this is my glory, this is my brilliance. Being a mother fits me like a good pair of jeans.

I wonder what Paige's little girl looks like? Does she think about stuff like that? Does she wonder if the big bright eyes she described to me were still liquid blue? Does she worry about what sort of parents raised her? Should I ask her? What is my role in this? Did she tell me so that I could help her find her child, or is she looking for some sort of absolution for a sin she thinks she committed? God, life is so tough. Wouldn't it be so great to find her daughter? Or would it...

Twenty-three

"The best way to predict the future is to invent it."
—Alan Kay

Paige

Jason chewed his cereal loudly, a habit that I once found endearing. Now, it struck me as rude and repulsive. For a distinguished guy, he has some "off" characteristics. His black hair was slicked back into its usual greasy sweep and his blue suit was free of crimps or creases. More than any day in the past two years, he looked content.

"So, you're good with this, right?" he said from behind the newspaper, oblivious to my glare.

Leaning on the kitchen counter, I stared out the window into our beautifully manicured yard. "I'm fine." The trees are fine, the yard is fine, your suit is fine, and everything is just fine.

"Good." He came to me and embraced me from behind. "I know you really wanted this, Paige, and so did I, but maybe it's just for the best. We're so used to being together, just the two of us, maybe this is the way it's meant to be."

"For the best," I repeat. We had come to a decision the night before to stop all treatments. Forever. No more doctors, no more tests. No baby in our future. Jason was the one to initiate the option of taking a break from it all, and although I felt like I was giving up my chance at motherhood, I knew my marriage had to come first. The stress of the endless tests had taken its toll on both of us.

"You know what they say—sometimes when you relax, it can happen. Let's try not to think about it, all right? If it's meant to be, it'll happen. If not, then so be it." Jason headed toward the door. "Have a good day, hon. And don't worry so much; we tried. I love you."

I was choking on his sentiments, all of them so very textbook, so dry. "Have a good d..." The door slammed before I could finish the sentence. I returned my attention to the window and noticed that the leaves had begun to change. Every year the leaves changed, fell off the trees and the snow came. Year after year the snow melted, giving way to daffodils and tulips. Everything changes, but nothing changes.

Hesitantly, I picked up the phone. She answered on the fourth ring. "Hi, Mom," I said. "It's me." *Why did I call?*

I could hear her choppy breathing, a byproduct of the twenty-odd years of smoking those extra long menthol-flavored cigarettes. My mother thought it gave her a Betty Davis kind of persona. "Is that you, dear?"

"It is. How are you?" It had been almost a year since my last phone call. A year. Most people talk to their parents every day, every week; at least once a month.

"I'm fine. I miss talking to you, dear. You haven't called." She breathed in deeply, the rattle sounding louder than it did the last time we spoke.

"You haven't called either, Mom; the phone lines work both ways. I get so busy with work, you know." I hated lying; I hated even more talking to her. *Isn't that awful?* And when I did, it was usually strained, which was why I didn't. No matter how often I called, or didn't call, it was always the same. "I don't want to fight, Mom. I just want to see how you're doing. I'm sorry it's been so long."

"Well, as good as can be expected, I suppose," she said. The beginning of a cough reached my ear, and I held the phone a distance away until the hacking and gagging was done. "Ever since your father left me, and the way my back aches, it's a wonder I can get out of bed. But I'm fine, don't you worry about me. And you?"

My parents divorced more than twelve years before and she still harped about it like it was yesterday. Never having worked a day in her life, it wasn't easy for her to be on her own. And I was long gone by the time my father left. She moved into a retirement community and loved it, although she insisted that she hated it—just because she could. "I'm fine, Mom. I called to ask you something." My stomach lurched, the morning coffee doing flips in my stomach. I took a deep breath, closed my eyes, and said, "Mom, I need to know about the baby."

I heard the familiar click of the lighter. "Baby? What baby, dear? Are you having a baby?" she said. "Good God, it's about time."

I could hear her inhaling and exhaling quickly. Quick puffs. As a child I thought it was sexy, the way she held the slender cigarette between two fingers. She was pretty and I thought she could've been a movie star. "No, Mom, I need to know about the baby girl, my baby girl." I lowered myself into the kitchen chair, resting the phone on my shoulder. More than a minute went by. "Are you there, Mom?" I said. "I want to know about her."

Raspy breathing. "Now why do you want to drag up bad memories for? Aren't we having a nice conversation?"

I took a deep breath. "Bad memories? I just want to find my girl, " I blurted out. My hands shook as I gripped the phone, cradled it to my ear with both hands. This woman was my only connection to what I needed. "If you know *anything*, please, please tell me."

There was nothing, not a sound, not a breath, not even a cough, for what seemed an eternity. The only sound was my heart beating so hard I struggled to catch my breath. "Paige," came my mother's voice, soft and crackled. "Do you have to dig this up after all this time? It's over with, so why not let it be? I thought you were going to make more babies, honey. You can make beautiful babies, you and Jake. You don't know what might happen if you…"

I interrupted her. "It's Jason, not Jake, damn it, I've been married twelve fucking years and you still don't know his fucking name!" My brow was wet and heat burned my cheeks. "I want to know about my baby, Mom. I *have* to know about her. Please."

"You don't have to yell," she said calmly. "And when did you start using that nasty word? I don't like it at all. It's so unladylike. All I can tell you is that a very nice family adopted her. Your auntie arranged it, one of those adoptions where you choose the family. I didn't know about their situation. They were all decked out in their Sunday best in that photograph they sent, so we figured they'd make nice parents. So many poor women couldn't have kids, I remember. Funny how that is, that some people can't have kids and others just pop 'em out left and right. Seemed like they would be nice people, as I recall. I never met them—so how would I know? They lived up there in California, so they had some money behind them. I don't know *all* the details and what I do know is kinda foggy. It was so long ago, Paige. You can't expect me to know. I can't remember."

Yes, I can expect you to know. You gave away my daughter, your granddaughter. You should know. "Do you remember their name, at least? A last name? Would Daddy know? Can you call and ask him?" My nervous stomach churned at the mention of his name. Daddy. The word didn't feel right on my tongue. I didn't have his number, I didn't know where he was, and I didn't care.

"I am *never* calling that man," she said, her voice quivering with emotion. "He left me, remember?"

"I know, Mom, but can you call him for me? You know I can't."

Silence again. "I'm sorry. You want to find out, you call him. I don't want any part of this. I'm sorry, Paige, I can't. I'm glad you're doing well. Better to just let it go, honey. Lord knows I have had to. It's always for the best," she said. "I have to go, they're serving up lunch and I think it might be lasagna. Augustine always puts her finger in it so I better get there before she does. I'm sorry, Paige."

I put the phone back in its cradle and laid my head on the kitchen table. In the darkness, behind my eyelids, she came to me. It's where she always comes to me—in the darkness.

***

"So, why don't you just call him?" Josie said, as she rolled two socks together and tossed them into the laundry basket. Christopher reached in, grabbed the clean pair, tossed them down the hall, and chased after them. Josie grinned. "You little turkey! Get back here with those socks!"

"Call him? Are you out of your mind?" I held up a pair of underwear with a large hole in the crotch. "Don't *tell* me that he wears these things! They are the most raggedy-ass pair of underwear I have ever seen in my life!"

"Hey," she grabbed the shorts out of my hand, giggling. "I told you, men are just men. He's a pig, what can I say? These are actually his best pair! Anyway, what can I do to help? And why can't your mom get the info for you?" Josie shook her head. "My parents weren't great either, but man, at least I could count on them."

I rolled my eyes. "I'd rather not communicate with either of them. Don't forget, I left home as fast as I could and I've never looked back."

Josie settled back against the couch. "How old were you again?"

Staring at the ceiling, I said, "Almost eighteen. Hard to believe it was twenty years ago." I sat next to Josie, our bodies slumped together on the couch.

"I never realized how alike we really were, you and me," said Josie. "Both of us left home in search of *something* and neither of us found it?"

I thought about it for a few minutes and put my hand on hers. "What were you looking for?"

Josie shrugged. "I guess I went in search of my identity." She laughed. "I know it sounds like a cliché, but it about sums it up. My parents weren't horrible, but it was my brother who was the hero in the family. I was pretty much a non-entity to them, the middle child. The boring child. Judith had piano lessons and ballet, and Keith excelled in all the sports. Me, I was a spectator. Until I took off and took control of my life. No more listening to Judy's screeching music recitals or sitting on some cold metal bleacher to watch Keith play another football game. I was finally doing my own thing and people were paying attention to me."

I tucked my legs beneath me. I always thought of Josie as such a strong person that I never thought of her as the kind of person who felt inadequate in any way. "That must have been rough. I always wanted siblings, when I was young. I always thought being an only child was the worst," I said. "It's too bad that you had to leave home so young. Did you really find what you were looking for, back then?"

The sound of clicking heels interrupted our conversation. Around the corner Christopher wobbled, wearing Josie's red high-heeled shoes and a pink scarf, his face covered in red lipstick. Josie leaned forward and smiled, her hand still on mine. "I didn't find it right away, but I did find it," she said, glancing at her son. "And you can, too. If you still want to."

Twenty-four

"Understand that the right to choose your own path is a sacred privilege. Use it. Dwell in possibility."
—Oprah Winfrey

Start Your Own Adoption Search For Just 50 Dollars a Month! (subject to small down payment). Looking For Your Birth Parents? Search No More! Call Us Now And Find Your Loved One Fast!

Setting the newspaper on the floor, I sat upright. I watched Jason through the front window, mowing the lawn in his normal pattern: down one side, across the bottom, up the middle, and back across in a straight line. He insisted it cut the blades of grass in a way that inhibited uneven growth and he spent hours reading up on the subject. Along with cooking, this was one of his favorite things to do. Sometimes I felt as if my husband's need for perfection fell short when it came to the woman he married. Maybe it was the way he fixed my hair when he thought it was out of place, or the way he corrected me when I mispronounced a word. Whatever it was, it was becoming increasingly obvious that I didn't measure up.

In the last three weeks, we had eaten dinner together a total of four times—he cited work responsibilities, business meetings, and phone calls as having priority over spending dinner with his imperfect wife. Maybe I was just being paranoid.

"He's never home, " I complained to Josie, while we were attempting to follow the Tae Bo master who was twisting this way and that and kicking his leg out. "I haven't talked to him about, you know, searching for—you know who."

Josie stopped and turned to me. "You know who? Geez, can't you even say it?" she said. Her brows furrowed into a perfect V. She inhaled deeply, her face softened. "Paige, what would you have named her? If mean, if you could have named her yourself."

I gazed down at the floor, my throat suddenly felt tight. "I've thought about it so many times, over the years. If I had been there, I would have named her Angel. It's what came to me when I saw her face: 'What an angel.'" I raised my head to meet her gaze.

Josie was smiling wide. She grasped my shoulders and squeezed. "Then find her! What are you waiting for?"

I was envious of Josie's zest for life, the way she rushed over hot coals fearlessly, while I tiptoed across each one, getting burned with every step. "I know, I'm pathetic. Who'd want such a pathetic woman as a mother?" Josie rolled her eyes. "It's terrifying to talk about her, like she's real. I have moments when I want to shout to the world about her, and then I want to curl up inside myself and pretend it never happened."

"What would she be now, around twenty-four?"

"Twenty-two, in about six weeks." I suddenly felt the reality of that, being the mother of a grown woman. But I had missed her first words, her first steps, and her first day of school—so many firsts. "I wonder if she's married, or in college or if she's—"

Josie cut me off. "Only one way to find out, kiddo." She handed me the newspaper. She had circled a bunch of adoption agency ads and information—lawyers, investigators, and the like. "You gotta start down the road if you want to get anywhere, so start."

Twenty-five

"If you haven't the strength to impose your own terms upon life, you must accept the terms it offers you."
—T.S. Eliot

I began the search for my daughter. Without the help of my parents, the chances of finding her were slim. It was a Wednesday. I know this because Jay played racquetball every Wednesday, every week. Same day, same time. Clockwork.

I wasn't put off by the difficulties that awaited me. I knew what I wanted, that it was the one thing missing in my life—the knowing. Was she alive? Was she happy? Even if she hated me for giving her away, I had to know what happened to the child I carried next to my heart.

"Where will you start?" asked Josie, having just arrived with her son and a pot of my favorite coffee. "I'm on pins and needles! I'm so excited for you."

I poured two cups, the aroma filling the air. Christopher busied himself with pots and pans.

"I think I'll start with the hospital."

Josie placed her hand on mine, rubbed it with her thumb. "It must have been awful, Paige, all these years. You never thought about finding her before now?"

I shook my head. "I blocked it out, denied it completely. Then I met Jason and you know the rest. I've read about moms who find their babies, but the kid is angry and doesn't want anything to do with them."

I had thought of these women, disappointed after years of sadness. Maybe it was one of the reasons I had avoided the issue. One of many reasons. "There's a lot I need to think about." I was so tired, hadn't slept well, with my mind racing. All those dark memories, carefully tucked away, were emerging. Having disturbed their hiding place, I was forced to look deep into their center.

"Is there something else?" Josie asked.

I sighed. "I guess it's like the wallpaper in your house—so many layers."

Josie nodded and said nothing. I loved this about her, the way she knew when there was more and gave me the time to let it out slowly.

"Layers, Jo, years and years of layers. Every night my mind goes back to that day, the day of the rape. I never saw anyone or talked to anyone about it. And my family—their main concern was keeping it secret." I closed my eyes and a picture flashed, bits and pieces of color, faces, shapes, darkness and then light, and my mother's face, clear as day, her smiling face looking down at me. I remember how my knees were tucked up to my chin and I was trying to make myself as small as possible. She was staring down at me, her brow crinkled.

***

The computer sputtered slowly to life. I was feeling much the same, unable to power up without effort. I scrolled down my list of web sites; there were plenty of places online where birth mothers gathered to share their stories. There were so many, in fact, that I wasn't sure where to start.

I went to one of the sites and typed in "searching for birth daughter." The screen came to life, listing dozens of agencies. I looked for something that fit, that might lead me in the right direction. I found message boards for adopted children looking for birth mothers, birth mothers looking for adopted children and hopeful adoptive parents and grandparents. And then I saw *California Adoption Search* and knew that I was on my way.

Twenty-six

"Life is a sum of all your choices."
—Albert Camus

"Paige! Hey, wake up, sleepyhead." I heard Jason's voice in the distance. It sounded as if he were talking through a long tube.

I sat up, confused, my eyes squinting as they adjusted to the light.

"It's eight o'clock," he said. "You must have been pretty whacked out—what did you do all day?"

I could tell by the inflection in his voice that he was irritated. I looked around the room—papers were on the desk, some were scattered about the floor. I could see the dishes from breakfast still lined the counter top in the kitchen. One of Jason's pet peeves: not doing the dishes right away.

I cleared my throat of sleep. "I was on the computer most of the day. Sorry. Time flies—" I smiled, Jason didn't.

"I thought you had clients today," he said, gathering papers off the floor. He held one up. "What is this?"

I had printed out all the information I could find on adoption, including reunions, their psychological impact, building a relationship, and so on. "I'm looking for my daughter." It was out. My chest expanded and I felt a wave of confidence come over me.

Jason stepped back slowly, as though I were suddenly contagious and he feared exposure. Without a word, he walked into the kitchen. I heard the refrigerator door open, the sound of wine being poured into a glass.

"Hey!" I shouted. "That's it, you just walk away?" I got up from the chair and found him sitting at the kitchen table. His face was blank. He took a sip of wine, swooshed it slowly in his mouth, tilted his head back and swallowed.

"Good wine," he said.

What an ass! I shook my head, pulled out a chair, and sat next to him. "What?"

"Some things get better with age…like this wine." He took another sip, ran his tongue over his teeth and savored its fruity flavor.

"I'm not in the mood for riddles. What the hell are you talking about?"

He set the glass down. "Some things are meant to be stored away, only to be savored when they age. Not so with kids. I don't know what on earth you think you can gain from this. Whoever she is, she's already lived a life without you. I can't imagine how it can help her if you go barging into her life. Did you think of that when you planned all this?"

I stared into his eyes. "Oh, no, Jay, don't you give me that! This has nothing to do with her; it's you. And I'm not surprised. I knew you'd react like this, I just knew it." I leaned over his shoulder. "You, Jason, are a selfish prick." I stepped back, feeling unsteady.

He swung around in the chair. "Nice word. Did you get that one from Josie? Your vocabulary has certainly grown over these past few years."

I breathed in deeply and my hands started to shake. "What in the hell are you talking about? Are you trying to piss me off?"

Jason took the bottle and filled his glass to the brim. "You wouldn't have even bothered with your past if it weren't for her. She's bad for you. Did she egg you on? Tell you some romantic story about how your daughter needs you? Needs to know who you are? Please. You're not only going to fuck up your life, but screw up her life, too!"

I blinked. "And yours." *That was what it was really about.*

Jason nodded. "Okay, yes, and mine, damn it. I thought we'd resolved everything. I thought we were happy—just the two of us." He stood and approached me. I backed away.

I nearly laughed. "What ever gave you the idea that I was happy? Perhaps the question should be: When have you ever asked me if I was happy?"

Jason seemed unprepared for that because his normally quick-witted response was slow in coming. "Does *anything* make you happy? Or are you the happiest when you're miserable?"

I stared at him, angry. "I'll see you later."

"What do you think you're doing!" he demanded.

I smiled. "I'm doing whatever the hell I want to, Jason. Get used to it."

***

The park on the corner was blanketed in darkness. The place was deserted. Maybe it was the adrenaline rushing through my body that warmed me, made me feel safe in this quiet place. It was totally out of character for me to be anywhere alone after dark. Jason knew that, he would worry. *Good.* I wanted him to worry about something other than himself for a change.

I sat on the swing, my legs dangling, and I pushed myself higher and higher. My hair blew in the wind, being flung back and forth as I pumped my legs to a new rhythm. It had been years since I had played in this park, too many years. The night was as quiet as a nun, the only sound my own *swoosh*, *swoosh*, *swoosh*. When I got as high as I could, I took a deep breath and jumped. I landed on both feet but my knees buckled and I tumbled onto the damp grass. I laughed out loud and stretched out onto my back.

The sky was a deep purple—my favorite color—and freckled with sparkling lights, some bright and some that seemed to fade away the more I stared at them. It was so peaceful here. I closed my eyes, trying to absorb the stillness. It had been so long since I felt at ease with life, with myself. I was tired of running. I had been running away from so much, for so long. It was time to stop and let it all catch up with me.

***

My mother was no help. I remember that day when she found me curled up on the bed. Without a word, she took me into the bathroom and turned on the shower. Hot. Burning hot. She guided me into the flow. I protested at first, saying it was too hot.

"You gotta get rid of the sin, Paige. You will endure. God will help you endure."

I remember seeing my blotched red skin in the mirror. I never cried. Not once, then or after. I put on flannel pajamas and joined my parents for dinner. It was the same as any other day: My father talked about how his employees were all lazy bums; my mother sat quietly, absorbing every word.

I could see that Daddy didn't know anything. Not yet. He didn't even know about the rape until after he learned about the pregnancy. They took me to the doctor and pressured him to abort the baby, but it was too late. At six months, the baby was almost fully developed. Daddy was furious and stormed out of the doctor's office, dragging me with him. My mother followed and remained silent. She carried her rosary beads in the pocket of her housedress and more than once I caught her rubbing them, rubbing so hard I thought the metallic pink color would wear right off.

Soon after that, I was on a bus to California. How would I know that I would never again see the disappointing gaze of my father's eyes? I was dead to him from that day forward.

Twenty-seven

"Life is what happens to you while you're busy making other plans."
—John Lennon

Did you know that yoga induced farting?" Paige asked. We were strolling through the mall, trying to get some exercise. I grinned. "No, I actually didn't know that." She continued to talk about yoga and how relaxing it was, but I was only half listening. My mind was on that conversation I'd had with Jason.

After my outing in the park, he had ignored me for a few days. That was how he punished me: Silence. That was how he showed his disapproval. It was as if he were waiting for me to come around to his way of thinking. He waited it out. This time, I wasn't budging.

"Are you ever going to talk to me about this?" I asked him. "And I do mean talk, not dictate."

His forehead crinkled. "Fine. Talk. I'm listening."

"Well, I just don't see why you are so upset with me," I started. "This is not a whim, Jason. It's very important to me. I wish you could understand."

He took a deep breath, exhaled loudly, and plopped onto the couch. "I don't know what to say, except that I wasn't counting on this." He twisted his wedding ring. "To be honest, I'm tired of all this chaos in our life. Jesus! Can't we have just one moment without the drama?"

I struggled to keep calm, to keep my voice slow and steady. "How does *your* life change because I want to find my child?"

Jason put both hands behind his head and leaned back, contemplating. "Well, for one, you'll be opening yourself up to this emotional roller coaster…and we both know you're shaky on this subject. Have you thought about the implications? If it doesn't play out the way you want it to, are you emotionally ready to handle the disappointment?"

I felt myself start to quiver and took a deep breath. "Of course I've thought it through." I needed him to understand the implications, that I might finally put some closure to a horrible chapter of my life. "Jason, do you have *any* idea what it's been like for me? Do you care? You have no idea what it feels like, carrying a child for nine months and then handing her over to strangers, never to see her again."

Jason grabbed my hand and tried to pull me down beside him. I moved to the other side, maintaining the distance I had already established. If I got too close, I knew I would fall into his arms and let him fix everything. Not this time.

"You know how fragile you are," he said. "I'm worried about you. I'm trying to understand; I want to understand."

I folded my arms across my chest. "But you can't, Jason, because even I don't understand. What else can I do?" I held back the tears, inhaled. "Okay," I said, wiping my tears on my sleeve. "Bottom line is that I'm doing this with or without your approval."

Jason looked as though I had slapped him in the face. "Fine, just leave me out of it."

"Whatever," I said. "Do whatever you want. She's my daughter and I have to know." I stood and walked out of the room. I was not going to let him see me cry.

***

Josie was still talking when we arrived at the food court. Christopher asked for a cinnamon bun.

"You can have a mini bun, okay?"

"'kay, Mommy. And Coke, please?" His little face crinkled in a pleading grin, eyebrows raised. "Please, Mommy."

Josie laughed and tickled him under the chin. "No Coke, big guy. Chocolate milk is the treat of the day. Any takers?"

"Awright," he said, and rushed over to order his pastry.

I watched him for a moment. "He's getting so big," I said, ordering coffee. "It seems like he grows an inch every time I see him."

"Isn't it amazing how fast they grow? It sounds like a cliché, but time really does fly when they're little." Josie ordered coffee and turned back to me. "I remember feeling like the baby days would never end. And now, here we are, talking about preschool."

I stared at the floor, imagining my own child and how she had changed. Was she blonde like me? Did she have that embarrassing space between her teeth that I had before my braces? Was she gawky when she was a teenager, or was she glamorous? Was she short or tall? Did her eyes change, or were they still that brilliant periwinkle blue that I imagined she had when she opened them? Was she happy?

"Earth to Paige," Josie called out. "Hello…are you with me? Our coffee is ready."

I reached for my wallet.

"It's on me. You get it next time." Josie collected her coffee and Christopher's pastry. "Come on, let's sit."

Before we were settled, Christopher began devouring the creamy icing on his cinnamon bun.

"Slow down there," warned Josie. "Or you'll be sick."

I watched them for a moment. "I envy you," I told her.

Josie looked up. "Huh?"

"I envy the things you've been able to experience with your son, and all those things you'll do together as he grows up." I watched Christopher lick the sugary frosting from between his tiny fingers.

Josie smiled. "Don't envy anyone, Paige. Envy is an evil emotion. I know what you're saying, but it's pointless to beat yourself up over something you can't control."

"If only I had done things differently, I could be you. I could be sharing a sticky cinnamon bun with my child."

"Come on, don't be so hard on yourself. You were a kid; it wasn't up to you. How is the search going, anyway?"

I told her how I had talked to several people who were searching for their own children and I had also enlisted the help of an agency. "I put my name on the birth mother list. If she's looking for me, she'll be able to find me." The expression on Josie's face was so caring, not like Jason. "It's a step in the right direction. I don't have anything to go on, so it's tough. When there's no name of the adoptive parents, no record of where they lived…nothing…."

Josie took my hand. "It'll happen—at the right time—and it'll all work out. I know you don't believe me, Paige, but I can feel it. You aren't ready to be a mom yet."

"What do you mean I'm not ready?" I felt the anger rush to my face. Who was she to tell me I wasn't ready? Me, whose biological clock was on fast forward? "What, there's a course you have to take? I've waited over twenty years and damn it, I am ready!"

Josie grabbed at my flailing hands, held them tight between her own. "Sweetie, all I'm saying is that you have to heal yourself before you can be a mother."

Our eyes locked and I searched for meaning in her words. "I don't know what you're saying."

"You have to deal with the past. Really deal with it, before you can begin this new future."

I lowered my head, hiding my eyes. She was right, I was flying from one thing to another; I was still running away. *Damn it!* I'd been searching the Internet for something that I knew in my heart I was not yet ready to face.

"I have the name of a really good therapist," said Josie. "We go way back." She smiled. "It might be a good place to start."

Josie knew I was wounded. I had managed to remove the bandage, but all those years…. the wounds were still oozing and painful. I was learning that the wounds that don't bleed often take the longest to heal. Never being exposed to air, they are left to fester.

"Let me think about it," I told her. "And I'm sorry I got so mad." I leaned across the table and hugged her around the neck. "How the hell do you know me so well?"

"I don't," she said. "And that's the whole point. I'd like to see you uncover some of those layers so we can both meet the real Paige."

Twenty-eight

"Forgiveness does not change the past, but it does enlarge the future."
—Anonymous

"So tell me about you, Paige. Why did you come to see me today?"

I was expecting Ann to be an older woman, so I was a little thrown when a young woman appeared and called me into her office. She had black hair tied back in a neat ponytail, thick dark eyelashes, and no makeup, except for a neat line of red lipstick—matted, not shiny. She was thin, too thin, and wore avocado green tunic pants.

I cleared my throat, suddenly aware that I hadn't even brushed my own long hair that morning. I had shoved the whole mess under a baseball cap and was out the door before Jason got out of bed. I had stopped for coffee at the drive-through window and then driven to the address I'd been given. I waited in the parking lot for the therapist to arrive. I was the only one in the lot. And suddenly I was in her office, facing her and about to reveal my life.

"I was raped when I was fourteen years old." I had said this so many times over the last while that the words hardly evoked an emotion in me. She wasn't shocked either. That is, her stony glance didn't shift at my announcement.

"And when it happened, did you talk to anyone about it?"

I shook my head. *Not about the rape, not about the baby…or anything. It never happened.*

"My parents thought it was best to move on. We never talked about anything in our family."

Ann was writing notes on a small tablet. I was seated on a love seat and she was at her desk, her chair swiveled so that she faced me. It wasn't at all what I expected, certainly not what I'd seen on television programs. The office was filled with family photos, medical diplomas, and inspirational plaques. The one I noticed first said: *Keep your face to the sunshine and you cannot see the shadows ~ Helen Keller*

I didn't want to dredge up the past, but I knew that there was no other way to move on. Those shadows were still lurking.

"That must have been extremely difficult, " she said.

Yes! I wanted to yell. Yes, it was damn difficult! It was bad enough that he raped me, but the silence made me feel like I was raped again—by my own parents.

I shifted, trying to find a way to explain how I felt. "It's very hard," I told her. "I've never really talked about the whole thing, you know, in detail. I guess I thought my parents knew best. What child doesn't, right?"

She nodded, smiled. "If you feel comfortable talking, Paige, I'm here to listen."

And you won't judge me? You won't tell me that I am soiled forever? You won't tell me that no one will ever love me, that I'm used?

My hands started to shake and the voice of my father boomed through my head. I put my hands to my ears, as if to stop the sound.

Ann leaned forward and put her hand on my arm. "It's fine, Paige. Slowly. We'll go slowly."

***

I must have slept a long time because long shadows decorated the walls of the bedroom. Jason was working late again and I had no desire to eat. When I had returned home, I needed to go over the therapy session again and again. The more I talked to Ann, the more comfortable I felt. She told me it was not uncommon for women who had never dealt with sexual abuse to feel the way I did. It was post-traumatic stress, or some other clinical phenomenon. It didn't matter what it was; it just felt so liberating, being able to talk to someone. Ann seemed so genuine. Although I knew this was her job, fixing people like me, she seemed to have enormous compassion. The way she touched my shoulder, the way she wrapped both hands around mine when we met—I love it when people do that. It makes you feel like they really want to know you. It's not your typical *how-do-you-do* handshake. And the eye contact. Someone once told me to always maintain eye contact when you're shaking someone's hand.

We talked about the rape. I told her how I had opened the door and how it really was my fault. If only I had listened to my father when he had said not to open the door to anyone. I told her how the man had hurt me, how he had taken me to the bedroom, my bedroom.

"I like your pink walls," he said. "I can see through your curtains at night, when it's dark, and I knew your walls were pink. You should never have anything but pink walls." He brushed a hand through my long blonde hair.

I thought I had stopped breathing, his voice was going on and on and I thought I had just stopped breathing. I willed myself to die, right then. My eyes closed, I prayed to God to just let me die…now. I wanted to turn back the clock and not open the door. If I shut my eyes long enough, maybe he would disappear?

I don't know what color the man's eyes were because I was too afraid to look him in the face. He pinned me on the bed with his knee; all his weight seemed to press down on my legs. He tied my wrists together, with my arms pulled over my head, behind me. I felt like my arms were being torn from their sockets. He tied another rope around my wrists and fastened the ends to the bedposts. When he was done, I felt the rope cutting into my skin. I kept my eyes tightly closed. If I didn't move, maybe he would leave. Maybe he was trying to scare me. Please don't hurt me. Please.

"Don't even think about screaming," he said. "I will come back here and I will kill your mother. She's almost as pretty as you are."

My heart pounded. I thought I might throw up. The more I wriggled, the more it hurt. He told me to lie still, that he didn't want to hurt me. He told me that he tied me up so I wouldn't run away, like the others. At that, I made a sound, not like a cry, not like a scream.

He pressed a hand over my mouth. "No noise, remember? Be a good little girl. You're a good little girl, aren't ya?"

My body started to shake. It began at my chest and then moved down my body, until the shaking became painful. I felt cold and my stomach twirled around and around. I remembered that if you kick a guy in his private area, you could really hurt him, so I tried to position myself to do this. I could smell his breath. It was hot on my face. I opened my eyes and saw that he was straddling me, one knee on either side of my body. He was leaning down, his face directly over mine. I wriggled my knees—I needed to get a good angle so I could hurt him—but he sensed it coming and slammed his hand down on my legs.

"I don't think so," he said. "Tell me, how come you never came to my place, huh? You always pass me by like you don't see me. Why?"

My eyes were locked on his now and I saw my own face reflected in his brown eyes. It was weird.

He started stroking my hair and I shook my head back and forth. His big hands felt heavy as he smoothed my hair all the way to the ends, brushing my shoulder and my breast with his knuckles.

I squirmed, wriggled from left to right. I tried to free my hands but the burn of the rope was too much. It felt like blood was trickling down my wrists. I felt like I couldn't breathe. The smell of him filled my bedroom.

Then, with one hand across my chest, he used the other to slide my shorts down to the ankles. I heard the sound of a zipper and then an intense pain. I screamed and he pressed his rough hand over my mouth. The hand smelled like cigarettes. I tried to move, but the weight was too much.

I concentrated on the light, stared directly at it, trying to burn my eyes. I tried to think of something else. I knew it would soon be over. The grunting sounds were slowing down. I was not a child. I knew what he was doing. I remember reading a story once about a woman who was raped by a stranger. It was over quickly, for her.

I started to cry, right there in Ann's office. I cried so hard my back hurt when I was finished.

"Just let it out," she told me, leaning forward and whispering. "Paige, it's normal to feel angry. It's normal to be upset with what happened. And it's *not* your fault." Ann handed me a tissue and I pulled myself together.

"I'm sorry," I told her. "I have never really thought about—well, not in detail, that is—the…the rape." As much as I wanted to keep that nightmare buried, it felt so good to let it out—even if doing so made it real.

"You do it however you need to, Paige. I like to let things evolve with my patients. I don't think there are two people I've encountered who heal in the same way. You'll find your way; I'm here to guide you through the tough spots. You'll be doing all the work."

I smiled and then replied, "Then maybe you should be paying me."

The day was done. It had been painful, recalling those memories, but I survived. What was more surprising to me was that I could recall every smell and every sound from that terrible day. I could still hear the sound of his voice, the feeling of his body on mine, and the searing pain when he entered me.

I thought about running over to tell Josie all about my session with Ann, but I didn't. This was possibly the first time in our four-year friendship that I felt the need to go it alone. Ann had told me to *excavate* and that was what I intended to do.

Twenty-nine

"We find comfort among those who agree with us—growth among those who don't."

—Frank A. Clark

The snow was starting to accumulate on the road and, as always, the small town was unprepared for its first storm. The wipers on my car flipped back and forth, a rhythmic squeak sounding every time they flipped left. I found myself absorbed in the beat: *swoosh, squeak, swoosh, squeak.*

The parking lot was almost empty and I pulled into the spot closest to the door. I loved to watch storms, but hated being in them. I'd been seeing the therapist for more than a month and I knew more about myself than I ever imagined I would. At first I thought I'd hate the experience, but then I found myself looking forward to our appointments.

"You are never going to believe this!" I blurted out, after Ann escorted me into her office. "I heard from the agency and they have a lead on a girl. She was adopted in California, it's the right hospital, the right day, and they said there are other things that lead them to believe it might be her. Isn't that amazing? I don't want to get too excited, you know, in case it's not her but…wow!"

Ann didn't say anything right away. I wanted her to tell me that it was great news. Instead, she pointed to the coffee maker, as always, and I shook my head.

"Aren't you excited for me?"

"Of course I am," she said. "I want to talk about it, it's exciting. But let's just start where we left off."

I nodded. I needed coffee. After pouring a large cup, I settled on the couch. "So, where were we?"

Ann flipped her black hair to the back. It was pin-straight and shiny as a new penny. "Why don't you tell me how your week has been," she said. "That is, other than the call from the agency. How have you felt about our sessions so far? Is the group therapy working out?"

I had started group therapy the week before and found it just okay. I was not excited about sharing my life with a roomful of strangers. We were five women and two men, and we met at the library across town. They had been meeting for more than six months, so I felt a little odd. Being the new member (seems too flip for the subject) of anything has never been my favorite thing. As a child, I was always more comfortable sitting at the back of the class. This group made a point of asking everyone to share.

"It's fine," I told her (although my voice said otherwise). "I don't know if I'll stick with it, but I promise to give it a Girl Scout effort. It just feels weird. They're nice and everything—" I stared at my feet. I wanted to move on to another subject, was anxious to talk about the adoption, but Ann was calling the shots. "It was an okay week. I worked a little and wrote in my journal, like you said. I'm not a great writer, so I hope you aren't going to critique it."

Ann smiled her bright smile. "Absolutely not. I won't even see it. It's yours alone. I find that people who write tend to be more open to sharing, so I always encourage my clients to keep journals. And you are liking it?"

"I never thought I would, but I have to admit it feels good to pour out my soul on paper."

"Have you written the one thing you would say to your parents, if they were here?"

"About the rape, you mean? Or the baby? Or what?" I had forgotten about last week's little assignment.

"It can be about anything."

"Well, I've spoken to my mother, so that's not much of an issue. But my dad—we haven't talked in years. He pretty much disowned me, like I said, after the baby came." I looked down and saw that I was wearing one red sock and one maroon one. That's what I get for dressing in the dark.

"And are you interested in talking with him?" Ann asked.

I immediately shook my head. "I have no desire to rekindle any relationship with him, if that's what you mean. He's an evil man."

"Does it bother you that you don't talk to him?"

I sighed. "I guess it bothers me that I can't have one of those sitcom-style relationships with my father, yes. I wish I could call him and tell him that I was looking for my child…or just tell him how I am, what I'm doing with my life. But he doesn't care. I've learned to keep my expectations of him within the realistic zone." I paused, remembering the day he discovered I was pregnant. "He told me long ago that I was no longer his daughter. He made it very clear that God was punishing me for my sins and that he didn't want to be brought down by my act of indiscretion. He told me that I would have to give the baby away, that I could live there until I was eighteen, and then I was out. No matter how I tried to convince my father that it wasn't my fault, he wouldn't listen."

"Don't tell me it isn't your fault. Don't tell me that. It's your body, isn't it? So why would you go around sharing it with the neighborhood, huh?" He grabbed me by the arm, shook it like he was trying to shake loose the truth. "Paige Marie, you are no longer a child of mine. You have disgraced me before God. You will never see this child, this blasphemous creature that you call a baby. It's a sinful thing you have done."

I flinched from a pain that stung after all these years. At the time, I believed every word he said. I believed that God had cursed me and that I was raped because He wanted me to learn something, a lesson. I spent so many years believing that the rape could have been prevented. Could it have been?

Ann leaned forward making eye contact with me. "You know that your father needed help, yes? And that he truly didn't know what he was saying. If there's one thing you get from our sessions, I want it to be that you are a good person and that none of this was your fault. I want you to think about all the good that you've brought into your life."

I nodded, trying to understand, and I sipped the coffee slowly, careful not to burn my tongue. But I wondered, what good *have* I brought into my life?

"Paige, some people believe that you can only rid yourself of this pain by talking to your father, but I disagree. I think you are strong enough to let go of all that guilt you've been carrying around. It's time to release yourself. You are the only one who can do that."

You are allowed to be happy, Paige.

I nodded, nursed my coffee. None of this was easy. "I left home and never looked back. Over the years, I watched people with normal, regular parents and I was so jealous. They say you can't miss something you have never had, but I don't believe it. I miss having a relationship with my dad, where we go to a baseball game or he comes and cooks in our backyard. As for my mom, we haven't talked much over the years. We're not at all close."

"Tell me more about your mom."

"My mom? She worshipped my dad—not much else to tell. He was her world, and I...well, I was the constant reminder of how she had let him down."

***

Josie was pulling into the driveway just as I got home. Her car's wheels were spinning as they ploughed through the piles of snow that had accumulated.

"Hey there!" I yelled when she got out of the car. "Hey!"

She turned and waved.

I made my way across the treacherous road and hugged her. "How are you?" It had been a whole week since we had gotten together. The last time we tried, she ended up canceling because Christopher was sick.

"I'm fine," she said. Christopher was already out of the car and rolling in the snow. He was the spitting image of his father. At four, he looked more like a six-year-old. "How are you doing?"

I smiled. "I'm great. Got a lead on a girl adopted from the hospital in California. It might be her. Wouldn't that be amazing?"

Josie's face lit up and she grabbed my coat. "Oh my God! I'll keep my fingers crossed."

I was staring into her eyes and they didn't look right to me. "Are you sure you're okay?"

She blinked. "Just the flu."

I nodded. "Ah, well then, go and rest. I've got to check my messages!"

I ran back across the road. When I reached my front door, I turned, but Josie was already in the house. I shook off a weird feeling and darted to the answering machine. Its light was flashing.

"Ms. Matthews, please call us at the Torkelson Agency as soon as you get this message. Thank you."

My heart began to pound. I dropped my bag on the floor, dialed the number, and introduced myself. "One moment please," said a receptionist, and then elevator music came on the line. All harps and violins.

"Hello, Ms. Matthews!" came the perky voice of the gentleman doing the search. "I have news for you."

My chest burned and my heart pounded so hard that I swear I saw my blouse move in and out. "Go ahead, I'm listening."

Thirty

"Every day brings a chance for you to draw in a breath, kick off your shoes, and dance."
—Oprah Winfrey

Josie

The parking lot at the doctor's office was packed, as usual. I swung into the first available spot and threw the car into park. Taking my hands off the steering wheel, I stared out the window, unable to move. I took a few deep breaths, but even that made me tired.

Since hearing the word *metastasis*, my whole world had changed. *Metastasis: transfer of a disease-producing agency from the site of disease to another part of the body.* It was not encouraging.

The doctors tried to convince me to continue with treatment, but I had other plans.

"What is the prognosis?" I had asked him straight out. "How long? And you know me, so don't sugarcoat it." He had cupped his chin in his hand, as if contemplating how to find the right words.

So, here I was. This was the last stretch. In a funny sort of way, I knew it was coming. Ever since I was a kid, I had this eerie feeling that my life would be a short one. Maybe that's why I concocted The List. Maybe I knew, in some strange way, that I had to do as much as I could, when I had the chance. And I did. I can't complain. In a very short time I have accomplished more than some women do in ninety years of life. I just wish that it could have been different. I don't know why I'm where I am, but I've stopped trying to figure it out. You know, live a good life and you get your just rewards. Although I'm not sure if I believe this anymore. Okay, so maybe I am a little pissed about the whole thing.

The words stuck in my head. "Less than a year, Ms. Ferguson. Without treatment, I can't say for sure." There it was: less than a year. Well, it's good to know *when*. Not such a bad thing, the knowing.

This visit was to be my last. Things had taken a downward spiral…fast. In just weeks I felt the changes in my body, felt like I was melting. Like the snowmen that Paige, Christopher and I make after every first snow. Even though you think they'll survive the entire winter, there is that one day when, in the blink of an eye, the snowman is reduced to a puddle.

I had already started to feel the heat.

Given my stubborn response to chemotherapy, the doctor suggested I take a couple of prescriptions home with me. I know he was trying, in a roundabout way, to tell me that it was only going to get worse. I'd been having terrible abdominal pain over the past few months and regular painkillers just weren't cutting it.

The waiting room was packed with cancer patients; not the happiest place on earth to be. Some were there for a follow-up, some for treatment, and still others had that panicked look on their face as they stared at the pasty-skinned people seated in the chairs around them. I had resorted to heavy foundation makeup; I wanted to keep looking like I was among the living. I was tired of the pity. Tom was a basket case, so I tried to look as normal and healthy as possible. I followed the nurse to the tiny room at the end of the hall. Other nurses smiled like mannequins as I passed; they all knew. I used to watch them give that smile to the other terminal patients, now it was my turn. The doctor came in just minutes after I settled into the chair tucked in the corner of the room.

"So, how are you doing?" he asked, flipping through the many pages of my chart.

"As good as I can be," I said. "Better than some, not as good as others."

"Anything new to discuss? Any concerns you want to go over with me?"

"Nope. Just give me the drugs, and fast." My lips curled into a smile. "I'm fine, but the pain is getting worse, like you said."

"Your weight is down a little." He raised his eyebrows.

This morning's weigh-in was a new low, 105 pounds. My weight loss program could give Jenny Craig a real run for her money.

"Finally, I can fit into my prom dress again," I said. He didn't smile. He was tugging on his bottom lip.

"Josie, are you sure you want to do it this way? I have to ask, because there are treatments," he said. "You could give yourself, and your family, more time."

I nodded quickly. "You got those prescriptions ready, Doc?"

He scribbled on a little pad and handed over the three prescriptions he had discussed during my last visit.

"These are refillable. Just call. Call if you need me." He crossed over to the chair, patted me on the shoulder, and was gone.

***

When Paige came barreling in the front door, she found Christopher asleep beside a mound of toy trucks.

"Hey!" she shouted.

"Hey yourself," I responded, adding "Ssshhh! He's knocked out in there." I pointed.

She grabbed my hand and dragged me into the kitchen. "You better sit down," she announced. "You are not going to believe this." She paced back and forth, wringing her hands. "They found her, Josie. They found my daughter. And they're sure it's her."

I saw a blue vein popping out on Paige's neck. It's such a miracle, how our bodies work, how blood runs through us, keeping us alive without our paying any attention. Without us realizing how much work it takes to keep that body functioning every day.

"Wonderful!" I told her. "God, that was fast. When will you see her? What's the plan?" I looked down at my clothes, sweat pants and a heavy sweater: my new camouflage.

"Not sure. But suddenly I'm so scared."

I wrapped my arms around Paige and she started to cry. She was trying to hide it, but I always knew when my friend was crying because she held her breath and then let go, her chest moving in quick repetitions.

"I'm sorry," she said, sniffling.

"It's huge, Paige. Of course you're emotional."

Paige pulled out a chair and sat down. I watched her face, knew that she'd been going through some heavy sessions with the therapist. She had never shared the details of the rape with me, so I was so glad she had someone to help her through it. All of the pieces seemed to be falling into place.

Paige suddenly looked at me. "Are you losing *more* weight? If you're not careful, you're going to fade away." This was the hard part, the lying. It killed me not to tell her that the cancer had returned, but I had my reasons. This was the one secret I would take with me. I have given it all up, until now, but this one—my dying—was going to be all mine. Sometimes misery didn't need company, and some things you had to do on your own. It was Paige's time to blossom; she seemed to be starting her life. Ironically, it was the same time that I was losing mine.

I knew I couldn't keep it up forever, but for now I had to. "Shit, I'm finally losing my baby weight and it's been four years!" And then I quickly changed the subject. "So, this agency news is exciting!"

Paige had her legs crossed, with one foot bopping up and down. "This waiting is the hardest. They asked a few more questions and now I just wait."

I had to wake up Christopher or he'd be up all night. I wanted to know more about this news, but I decided to push Paige out the door. The pain in my shoulder was excruciating. When I apologized for throwing her out, she hugged me.

"Oh, no, it's fine. I need to get back because Jason's friend is coming by to pick up a cookbook he borrowed…or something."

I nodded, knowing that everything we have in life is borrowed. Especially time.

Thirty-one

"Even the fear of death is nothing compared to the fear of not having lived authentically and fully."

—Frances Moore Lappe

I was halfway between that place just before sleep—when you are not sure if you're dreaming or not—when I realized that the phone was ringing. My eyelids were so heavy I couldn't tell if it was day or night. Must be the drugs. I heard a rustling in the room and tried to speak.

"Josie. Josie, you awake?" I heard Tom's voice. It sounded like he was in a tunnel. "Jo?"

"Hmmm," I mumbled. He leaned down closer and I could smell his new cologne. It was the expensive kind he said he wanted and I saved my loose change for months so that I could buy it on the sly before Christmas.

"Hey. Hon, I gotta go. Are you awake? Your sister just called and I told her to call back in an hour."

I rolled over, away from the sound of his voice. "I'm up, I'm awake. Where ya going?"

He came closer and kissed me on the cheek. "I've gotta go in for an early shift. I switched with Steve, remember? Babe, I really think I should call Paige; have her come over to give you a hand." He snapped on the light.

My eyes popped open. "No! I'm fine. Don't. Don't call anyone. I'm up." The room was spinning a little and I lay back down on the pillow. "I'm fine. Where's Chris? Chris!"

"He's watching cartoons. I gave him breakfast, but I gotta go. I'll call you at lunch, okay?" He went out the door and left the bedroom light on. Just in case I thought about drifting off again. It was getting harder and harder to get up.

I pulled myself to a sitting position and knew at once that it was going to be another tough day. The medication was helping with the pain but it made me so sleepy. My sister had called eighteen times last week just to be sure I was awake when I needed to be. *Damn Tom for telling her!*

"Josie, she's family, it's not right. You have to tell her and stop being a martyr, for Christ's sake," he said, after I got off the phone with her. "And you know what, your best friend is going be major pissed off when she finds out you've been sick all this time and didn't tell her."

I shrugged. "I don't care, she's got stuff to do. People have things to do, Tom. When I got sick, she dropped everything for me, and I appreciated it. But now she's got to live her own life and I have to live the rest of mine, my way. I don't care if you understand." *And I know she'll be pissed.*

In the kitchen, I struggled with the coffee pot. Shit! He could've made the damn coffee!

"Mommy!" Chris threw his arms around my thighs. "Come on, the *Battle Boys* are on."

"You know we don't let you watch that, so go find another show."

Note to self: Remind Tom about violent programs.

The detailed index I was creating for Tom included everything having to do with our son—things he had no clue about. Every day I remembered something else that needed to be added: allergic to penicillin (this was a biggy); hates broccoli; cannot sleep without his blue doll that my sister gave him—the only gift she ever gave him that was appropriate; needs closet door shut when he goes to bed (monsters live in the closet); still sucks his thumb (remove it after he's asleep); won't wear overalls; best friend's name is Paul Johnson (lives in Orchard Park, phone number highlighted in pink address book). There was so much to tell. I kept the list on the counter so I could scribble thoughts as they came. Lately, however, these thoughts seemed to flee my mind as quickly as they came. Once, when Paige dropped by, she saw the list.

"What's it for?" she asked.

"Oh, that. Well, I was thinking about going to visit Judith for a couple of weeks and I wanted to be sure Tom had everything he needed."

She didn't flinch. She was so absorbed in her search for her daughter; she was oblivious to many things. It was nice in a way. She was easier to fool.

The calendar on the kitchen wall caught my eye. Every month I had been tearing off a page, anxious to start a fresh new sheet. I would plot my days—dinner with Paige, Nail Works appointment, Tom's B-day, and so on. And then it dawned on me that those days will never again exist, so I stopped tearing them off. I think I was holding on to them—the days, weeks, and months—as tightly as I could. Sometimes that calendar made me feel like an outsider, watching my life ebb away. The calendars, the yearly subscriptions to magazines, the monthly utility bills, these were all tangible reminders that my days were numbered. *How morbid.* I tried not to obsess about it, but there were moments when I felt an overwhelming sadness. The grief wasn't so much for me, but for everyone else, everyone whose calendars would be forever changed by my death. Each of them would have to add another special day to their list of dates to remember. How sad for them. Mostly, I thought about Paige and wondered just how mad she really would be, missing out on the end.

***

I put the journal down and stretched with caution. The clock on the VCR was flashing 12:00, so I flipped on the TV to get the time. It was after four; Tom should be getting home soon. I was grateful for that, because I was finding it harder and harder to manage and it was really pissing me off. Worst of all, I was starting to act and feel like a sick person and I hated it. Soon, however, there would be no hiding it.

Paige had tried to call. Her number showed up on the call display.

In fact, there were fourteen calls from her in the last few days. I was spending a lot of time in the living room and I watched her come and go. From my vantage point, her life seemed to be on fast forward, while mine was winding down. Probably something to do with her daughter. Sounds so strange, saying *her daughter.* I was so happy for her. At the same time, I felt a terrible pain, just thinking about what I was missing, not answering her calls, not making time to see her. She had come so far and I knew that this would be a life-changing experience. The timing couldn't have been better. She was so wrapped up in finding her daughter that she likely had less time for me. For that, I was grateful.

I picked up the journal and scanned the last entry:

I am getting weaker a lot faster than I thought I would. I don't regret the choices I've made. I don't believe in regret, you know that. In the end, it's just a matter of choice. It may be the wrong choice for some, but for me, it feels right. And contrary to what Tom thinks, I am not trying to be a martyr. I truly just want to spend these last months reflecting on my life, and being with my husband and my son. That's a good choice. I don't want the treatments to kill me, eat away at my insides; the cancer is doing a good enough job on its own. I think I've come to like the cancer. It wakes you up. When they told me there was a chance of recurrence, for whatever reason that I forget now in my current state of mind, it got my attention. Even after months of chemo, there was still a chance that it could come back in some new form: in the bones, the liver, the lungs or the brain. Knowing that, all this time, was like the beginning for me. And here I am.

Before all of this started, I had a five-year plan and a ten-year plan. I put my nickels in a jar beside my bed so I could buy that beach house when my body and mind slowed to the rhythm of the ocean. Now, I'm going to die and all of it means nothing. I know that sounds morbid, but it's the truth. I planned for a future and now I'm going to die without having one. I'm okay with it—the dying. I'm not thrilled about it, but it's the new plan. I mean we are all going to die one day and I guess I'm glad that I had the opportunity of knowing, that it's all spelled out for me. It's a funny thing, the knowing. You just look at things in such a different way—when you know. As corny as it sounds—and I know it sounds corny—you really do stop and smell the roses when you know it may be the last season you see them bloom. It all seems so much more fascinating, now.

So I get to imagine the reality of my life ending, set in place all the things that will carry on after I'm gone. As scary as that sounds to you, it's a very reassuring thing for me. To be able to put everything in its place before I'm gone is such a gift. I've ordered the calendar for next year (the one that always hangs on the wall, from Avon) so that it will be familiar. Familiar will be good, I think, for Tom and Chris. Normal. I am trying hard to plan the days (after) so that it will feel like I'm not even gone. Well, you know what I mean. Of course, I'll be gone, but the sameness will be good, I think. Don't you? If I've forgotten any of it, I know that Tom will ask you. You know all of my routines. If you can order the Christmas tins from the Boy Scouts every year when you order yours, that'd be great. Tom loves those damn fruitcakes and he won't have a clue where to get them. I have a list but you know he'll lose it by the time the next Christmas order comes around.

When I started this journal a few years ago, I never really thought it would end, not like this. And I really never thought I would be using it to share my last days with you, Paige. I thought there would be a happy ending. But it shouldn't surprise you that I would continue to keep this journal. You of all people know that I have lived consciously, and so will die consciously. It's why I'm not afraid. I have learned to face my death as I faced my life—at full speed! I hope you can continue to do the same, now that you've figured out how to get started. I'm so proud of you for following your heart and searching for your child, no matter what.

I know there were times when my full-speed-ahead antics frightened you and that made me love you even more. You created a balance in me that I couldn't have found if we had not been friends. I know that some people have said, and will say, that I am just stubborn, and I know you are going to be so damn mad when you find out I have known about this for so long. There will be others who will be angry with me for not sharing this news with them, too. I want you to be the one to explain it. After all, you know me best. It will take you a little time, but I think that you will understand why, if you think about it.

Don't be angry. Anger is a wasted emotion. I tried to be angry at the cancer, way back when, and it made me more tired. Be happy. I am, almost. I can't change it, so I have to be. Besides, it's not the end, according to all those Sunday morning evangelists. Ya think? Oh, God I hope it's true. I'll send you a sign when I find out. Let's see…if there's truly a heaven, next spring you will have the greatest garden on the block. I know you'll appreciate that! Here's hopin'!

Okay, back to the friendship, because this is the story of an immortal friendship, it's not just about me. It's about us. Of course, it didn't start out as that, but I believe that the bond we share will reach far beyond my grave. Quit crying and just listen up for a minute. You are in my soul, girl. Don't you ever forget it. I'm just getting a head start, 'cause you know I'm not going to let you off the hook that easy. I'll be waiting for you, with margaritas on ice. Think about it; in heaven, the margaritas will be calorie-free. In the meantime, keep an eye on my boys for me, could ya? Tom has it all under control, but if Christopher needs to talk to a woman about say, his first girlfriend, or about someone who is bullying him at school, please don't let him turn to Judith! I beg you!

Okay, I don't want to get too mushy, but remember when we met? I was a crazy new mom who stayed busy with one thing or another, hiding from my feelings. Remember that ridiculous tartan dress I was wearing? Eek! I think I still have it! Remember how I told you how I dealt with emotions? "Emotions? So how do I deal with emotions, you ask? Well, it's easy, really, I ignore them!" After we got through the layers, you helped me to see that it was fine to be a tiny bit vulnerable. You softened me, Paige. You gave me the freedom to feel all of the emotions, good and bad.

There's something so great about having a best friend. I never realized how much I had changed because of you, until I read some of the early entries in this journal. I led a pretty wild life, and I don't know if I would have settled into motherhood as easily as I did, if not for you. You tamed me, girl! It's quite the accomplishment. You can ask my sister, if you don't believe me.

I am signing off for today. Time to pop a pill. I'm not going to share the gruesome details of the illness; it's the living that matters. Paige, it's always been the living that matters. You are going to make a helluva mom, girlfriend, you know. I'll be watching.

Thirty-two

"And in the end it's not the years in your life that count. It is the life in your years."
—Abraham Lincoln

The number for the hospice was tucked inside my wallet. Until today, I hadn't even thought of looking at it. But it started to feel weird when I breathed, like I couldn't inhale deep enough, and the doctor thought I should go in for a break. I don't know if he thought I'd buy into that explanation or not, but I knew the time was near. I also knew that, eventually, I'd have to stay in the hospital for good. The thought of it made me dizzy and nauseated. As much as I accepted the reality of my own death, I was still scared for those I was leaving behind. That was the unfairness of it all. Damn it. I thought I'd be ready.

With so much to do, I had spent the week organizing everything. Social Security card, birth certificate and life insurance, they were all in an envelope. I had even put in a brochure from a local cemetery, although I left the rest of the plans up to Tom. He didn't want to discuss it, but I needed to make it easier for him—when it was all over. He would have enough on his mind and I did not want Judith putting in her two cents.

"But you have to get married again," I told him one night, when I was trying to get him to talk about it.

"Jesus, Jo, do we have to do this now?" He was rubbing my back with oil. My skin had become so dry.

"When would you like to talk about it?" I asked. "Never," was all he could say, and then he left the room. I felt so bad for him. If I could spare him this, I would. Some people with terminal cancer take their final destiny into their own hands. I've read many stories about conveniently taking too many pills, or finding ways to choose the time for their demise because they wanted to spare their loved ones the agony of watching them slip away. I couldn't do that.

On my dresser were the envelopes, all of them addressed and ready. One for Paige, one for Tom, and another for my son. I tried not to think about that last one. It was the only time I doubted, even for a second, not choosing the heavy-duty treatments offered to me.

According to the message on my machine, Paige had left town. I saw her a few weeks before she left. She noticed my gaunt complexion, but I feigned stomach flu and shooed her away, so as not to catch it.

"Hey," said her message. "Where the heck are you? I came by the other day and the door was locked. Hope you're okay, 'cause your car was in the driveway. You can't still be sick with that flu. You've really had a tough time of it. I think you better talk to the doctor about some vitamins for your immune system. It might be compromised. Anyway, call me as soon as you get this. I'm going to see her, Jo. I can't wait to tell you all about it. We talked on the phone for over an hour! She's great; she's really great. She just lives in Kansas City, so I'm driving. Yes, driving all the way there by myself. I'm so excited, I hope she likes—" The answering machine cut her off.

I was so proud of her, driving all the way to Missouri by herself. Boy, she had really come a long way. Paige was going to be just fine.

***

Paige had been gone a week when I received her letter.

Dear Josie,

Hello from Kansas City! I arrived safe and sound, believe it or not. I tried to call you but I keep getting the machine. There's just so much to say! I was going to stay at a hotel, but she, my daughter, insisted that I stay here, with her. Isn't it wild? I have a daughter. She's tall, yeah; she's tall! She's blonde and beautiful and perfect. Her name is Christina. Isn't that a wonderful name? She's married, and *she's pregnant with her first child. Yes, I am going to be a grandmother! Can you believe it?*

The whole thing has been overwhelming for both of us—her finding out I was looking for her, and me finding out she was looking for me. Oh, I forgot to tell you that. She has been looking for me. I'm sorry that I have been such a distant friend lately. I'll make it up to you, I promise. You know, if it weren't for you, this never would have happened. I wouldn't have taken the risks that I've taken over the past few years. You have changed my life and when I get back—and I can't tell you when that will be—we're definitely going to have to pick up where we left off.

I can't wait for you to meet her. She can't travel just yet, with the baby due and everything, but I have told her all about you, about us. She can't wait to meet you and your family.

Oh, I guess I should tell you that she was adopted by a nice family, like I had hoped, but they never told her anything about me. She was raised in California, but moved out here to the Midwest to go to school. She's a pharmacist! We've spent a lot of time talking, trying to keep it positive. I haven't shared too much about the details of her father—not sure what to do about that—but we have just tried to get to know each other.

Everything in due time, I suppose.

How are you? Thanks for pushing me to find her, and to find me. Thanks for being there for me when I thought I was going to lose my mind. You're such a great friend, Jo.

Can you check in on Jason for me? I left food in the fridge and he can manage, but I'm not sure he knows where the washing machine is!

Signing off for now.

Love you and miss you,

Paige.

P.S. I will be back next month. I've cancelled all my appointments. This is where I need to be right now. Christina is having a hard pregnancy and I am going to stick around to get her through the morning sickness. I'm feeling like a real mother already! I'll write again or try to call. I left the number on your machine; so maybe when you get a chance, give me a call.

My eyes filled as I read the letter. It was so obvious how happy Paige was. Finally, she was complete.

Just as I was about to curl up with Christopher to watch a movie, the doorbell rang. "I'll get it!" he yelled, making it to the door before I could pull myself off the couch. He yanked it open and Mrs. Stewart was standing there holding a very large basket in her arms. I could barely see her face.

"Josie, dear, how are you doing?" She walked right in and deposited the basket onto the kitchen table. "I have been worried sick about you, dear."

I didn't know what to say. She walked through the house, picking up a sock, straightening and primping. "I told you to call on me, anytime. Why didn't you?"

I sat down on the couch. "I really didn't need any help then, Mrs. Stewart. How did you know?"

She came over and sat beside me. "It was Tom, and I have to say, dear, I wish you would have told me. You know I want to help."

Mrs. Stewart was a sweetheart, but the woman was old. She didn't need to be picking up after me! "Thanks," I told her. "Please don't be angry, but I didn't want anyone to know. She doesn't even know." I tilted my head to the right and Mrs. Stewart looked out the big picture window toward Paige's house.

"Well, now," she announced. "Why don't you just get yourself into bed and Christopher and I will make some popcorn. Go on, and I won't take no for an answer. Besides, you are much too weak to throw me out! So go and get some rest."

Leaning on the arm of the chair, I hoisted my body up from the couch. Waiting a minute to steady myself, I smiled at her and said, "Thanks."

Thirty-three

"It is not length of life, but depth of life."
—Ralph Waldo Emerson

Tom and Christopher had just left the hospital. I was glad they were gone; I hated that my baby had to see me hooked up to intravenous tubes and lying around in a bed. It must be so strange for him.

On the drive to the hospital, a few days ago, I noticed so many things I hadn't noticed before. The trees blew by, still dormant, as though waiting patiently for the days when they could bear new fruit and sway in the gentle spring breeze.

The painkillers were doing the trick and I passed much of the day drifting in and out of wakefulness. I was at the point where I welcomed sleep, the prelude to my final slumber, and it was while sleeping that I dreamed the stories of my life. They was always colorful, my dreams. Purples and coral pinks were the backdrop to the place where I felt well and content. There was no pain in my dreams, no one shedding tears in dark corners of my home when they thought I couldn't hear them.

In my dreams, Paige and I sat on the front porch, cracking up about Tom's latest mishap, or recalling a dirty joke we'd read on the Internet. In my dreams, there were no secrets. There was no need for them. There was no pain and no disappointments. No regrets. No need to shelter each other from that harsh reality, that life didn't always serve up exactly what we ordered.

Dear Paige: It's getting harder to write so this is my last entry. The rest of your story is yet to be told. It's our story now. I was there when you found your life and I hope you continue to live in authenticity to your true being for many years to come. Remember that in the quiet rhythm of your life, my heart will always beat right alongside yours, my friend. I'm leaving my heart and this journal with you, so take good care of them. There's so much more to the story, so tell it well.

Josie

Epilogue

"Don't be dismayed at good-byes. A farewell is necessary before you can meet again. And meeting again, after moments or lifetimes, is certain for those who are friends."
—Richard Bach

She's beautiful, isn't she?" I said to Christina, as I placed the small photograph of Josie and me by my friend's gravestone.

Christina must have taken that as a sign that she could interrupt my talk with Josie, because she said, "Yes, she really is. I wish I could've known her."

I put my arm around my daughter. "So do I. And you will."

Because I will tell you every last detail of our short time together. I will tell you how she was the strong one and how much she wanted me to find you. I will tell you how she was the only one who knew how to make me laugh until my sides ached in pain. I will tell you how we were—Josie and I. You will know her. Us.

"I can't even begin to tell you how mad I am that she didn't tell me about this."

Christina rubbed my shoulder. "She must have had her reasons."

***

A year after your death and still wake up, my pillow wet with tears. Grief is like that, I suppose. It doesn't follow a particular pattern—never the same for two people. Some days I still can't believe you're gone. The wind rattles the door and I expect to find you standing there on the other side, wearing one purple sock and one green, holding on to some new treasure that you discovered at a garage sale. But you'll have a matching purse at your side.

Jason has decided to take some time off, from me, from us. It's for the best. I am happy that he followed his heart and I need to follow mine. Life is short and I plan on enjoying every minute of it. The house is for sale and I may be moving out to Kansas City. I'm so excited.

My daughter is pregnant with her second child. Can you believe it? I am in love with my first grandchild, a boy, and now I will have a granddaughter to spoil. Christina is naming her Ivy. And so it goes, Jo. My life is unrecognizable today; the empty spaces filled with more love than I ever thought I deserved. I keep your picture on the visor of my car. When I take that exit ramp to the freeway, I know that you're watching, applauding me. And every time I reach my destination, I look up and you're still there.